A CHRISTMAS WRAITH

A Specters Anonymous Novel

PHIL BUDAHN

Phil Budahn's
Specters Anonymous
Novels

CHAPTER

iny Tim limped across the shabby rug toward a bowl on the table. Shadows drooped across the stage like played-out emotions, unable to muffle the patter of his ever-hopeful heart.

Soon the little scamp would have more to worry about than an empty porridge bowl. I could personally vouch for that.

My pal Hank balanced on the edge of his seat.

"When's the Ghost of Christmas Past making his appearance?" Hank whispered, keeping his eyes on Tiny Tim's tottering last steps.

"Any second now," I whispered back.

"The tension is killing me," he said.

"Shouldn't you be past that?"

Inches now from the bowl, Tiny Tim raised on his crutches to peek inside. I knew it was crazy, that I shouldn't care, that the game was rigged – and, by the way, I was the one who rigged it – but despite countless rehearsals, part of me still rooted for the little guy to get lucky.

"Mayhaps," says Tiny Tim, "mayhaps, I shall find a wonderful surprise this glorious Christmas morning." Eyebrows arched and lips trembling in a hopeful smile, he was leaning over the table when a head popped from the bowl and said:

"It's showtime, folks!"

As heads go, this one had seen better nights. The hair was a shade of grayish-red and splayed like a bomb blast; the jowls jangled, the wild gray eyes wobbled, creating the impression of an overmedicated grandmother who discovered a spider in her soup.

Hank shot me a scowl. "You're slipping, Ralph."

I answered with a shrug. Don't you hate it when you're trying to be sneaky and someone outsneaks you? I hurled a scowl into the orchestra pit at Fast Eddie; he was trying so hard to be casual I almost expected to see a sign hanging from his neck that said: *Don't even ask.*

"Come on, boys," Fast Eddie hooted at the actors, even the ones who couldn't hear him. "Let's see who still has some backbone left."

Tiny Tim inched away from the table on the stage, unaware of either the head in his porridge bowl or the commentary from me and my friends in the audience.

"What an innovation," Veronica rose from the seats behind me. "Just what this play needs. A pickled amateur who can't remember her lines."

The head in the bowl popped up. "I heard that. Who called me an amateur?"

"I did." Veronica said.

With a resolute fix to her lips, Veronica made her way down the aisle to the stage. Her hair hung like a chain-mail scarf atop her tall, lean figure.

The head in the bowl – whose owner was named Esmerelda, a newcomer to my neighborhood – lost control of her eyeballs as they skidded around her sockets like a pair of frantic comets.

Fortunately for dramas on all planes of existence, a director was present.

"All right, people, let's take a five-minute break." A svelte young man with a sweater slung over his shoulders scurried up the steps from the orchestra pit, his hands patting together noiselessly.

Esmerelda scooted down in the bowl to peek over the rim. Fast Eddie mumbled something about our theatrical community not having the talent to staff a mediocre fun house.

"Keep your focus, people." The director zeroed in on Tiny Tim. "Was a barracuda about to lunge out of that bowl at your nose? I don't recall anything in the script about barracudas."

Tiny Tim grew like a magical beanstalk, rising from his knees until the director barely reached his chin. Pointing a crutch at the table, Tiny Tim said, "I have a bad feeling about that bowl. It's evil."

"Save the spooky-wooky stuff for Halloween," the director said. "We're rehearsing *A Christmas Carol* here. I want to see goodwill and squalor, people. Goodwill and squalor."

From the bowl, Esmee hiccupped and, if I'm not mistaken, winked at me.

"Spooky-wooky, indeed," I muttered.

2

CHRISTMAS IS COMING. Front doors have broken out in wreaths. Colored lights blink from roof gutters and sparkle on the hedges lining every porch. Even on my level of reality, there's an interest in seeing one more production of Charles Dickens's holiday classic.

What do I mean by *my level of reality*? It's the one with me, Esmerelda, Hank, Veronica and Fast Eddie, but not Tiny Tim, the director or the stagehands. It's the place I appeared after reaching my expiration date, powering down, folding my cards, unplugging my neural hard drive, being the guest of honor at a funeral, and accepting that I'd become a spook.

Other than checking ghost stories like *A Christmas Carol* for accuracy, I don't pretend to be an expert on matters theatrical, unlike, to cite a random example, Veronica, now closing the distance with Esmerelda.

Esmerelda is more commonly known as Esmee. Her biggest challenge on most nights was avoiding the places that figured into her first life. If a spook made a connection with her previous existence, she wasn't likely to transcend to the deluxe regions of the afterlife.

Esmee's eyes grew wide as Veronica hauled an aura of righteous severity down the aisle. Esmee struggled to pretend she didn't see a stagehand scurrying forward with costumes in both hands until he passed through Veronica.

Veronica stuttered to a halt, clenched her spectral teeth and screwed her eyelids together. *Icky* is a strange word from a spook like me whose bones are lying under the ragweed somewhere, but icky is the precise term for what Veronica must've felt when that stagehand's pancreas and spleen sloshed through her.

Esmee howled with glee and slapped her thighs which, by the by, still needed support hose. "Come on, old girl. Don't tell me you're afraid of a warm-bodied male."

"If you knew anything about the afterlife –" Veronica began.

"Look out," Esmee gasped. "The whole fraternity is coming at you now."

Veronica despecterized so quickly that molecules of air snapped into place as they adjusted to her departure.

Time for me to get involved. Drifting from my seat, I shook my head. "I don't want to admit it, Esmee, but Veronica has a point. You shouldn't be here."

"Aw, what's wrong with a girl having a little fun? It's only a harmless prank. That nitwit with the pulse" – She pointed at Tiny Tim – "might as well be a lump of coal, for all he cares about us."

"Yeah, Ralph, why don't you explain why we shouldn't horse around?" Hank rested his chin on the back of his chair, enjoying himself entirely too much.

"Okay," I said. "But first let's talk about friends who don't do what they agreed to do."

Lest Fast Eddie have any doubt about the friend I had in mind, I gave him my best bug-under-the-microscope glare. Fast Eddie turned to Esmee for help.

"Don't be cranky with Fast Eddie," she said from the stage. "He knew I had this dream. Call me foolish, call me mad. But I'm drawn to the theater. Who is Fast Eddie to stand between a girl and her destiny?"

"She said she'd rip my head off if I tried to stop her," Fast Eddie added.

I hoisted my own head off my neck and tucked it under an arm, saying. "And your problem with that is?"

Fast Eddie had promised to recruit a biker from Heck's Angels to roar out of Tiny Tim's porridge bowl on an astral Harley, and I was going to hold Fast Eddie to that commitment.

Wisely, he accepted that he had some explaining to do. "Sorry to let you down, Ralph. But Dawkins told me he had the perfect candidate for this gig. I didn't know he'd pick Esmerelda."

"Dawkins, smawkins," I said, returning my head to my shoulders. "We've got to come up with something. Unless we want to run the risk of – "

I let my voice trail away. I didn't have to finish the sentence, not with Fast Eddie. He'd been around the cemetery a few times, he knew the score. A theater filled with the afterworld's finest is a tough audience on any night, not the crowd anyone wants to disappoint. But who can control a spook like Esmee who thinks being dead is just a cheap excuse to get sympathy?

Still, there are rules. And, of course, that was the answer.

I gave Esmee my best used-car-salesman smile as she glided toward me from the stage. "How'd you like to play a game?"

Esmee was on me like paint on a brush. "I could go for a few hands of poker. I'm feeling lucky tonight."

"Sure, we can do that," I said. "The thing is, you'll have to stop being an actress. It's someone else's turn to come from the bowl."

Esmee's lower lip quivered. Subtlety doesn't have a chance when that kid wants to pout.

"But I'm having fun."

"You've had your chance. Now you've got to let someone else play actress."

Esmee's eyebrows arched so high I thought they might shift to a nicer face.

"Do I get to deal?" she asked.

"'Natch," I said. "But first we've got a little detour."

CHAPTER

*H*ank and Fast Eddie joined us — Hank as backup and Fast Eddie for entertainment — as I led Esmee at astral speed to a hill on the eastern edge of Richmond where the streets were lined with trees and battery-powered candlesticks shined from most windows.

Esmee wore a skeptical look when we settled on the well-tended lawn of a church and headed down the concrete steps that led to the basement. A manic light gleamed in her eyes as she surveyed the building.

"I thought they only played bingo in these places. Glad to hear they're branching out. Gotta keep up with the times." She charged the steps, hit the cement bottom and kept going into the concrete. Which isn't as unusual as it sounds if you're new to the afterlife.

"Do you want to make sure she doesn't end up in Australia?" I asked Hank.

"Nah," he said. "If they can handle kangaroos, they're ready for Esmee."

So much for getting help from Hank. I could spend all night wandering through the tectonic plates. Before I reached the last step, however, Esmee respecterized in the basement room.

"Are you sure she's ready for this?" Hank asked.

"One way to find out."

ESMEE HAD BEEN barging lately through the hereafter like a loose spectral cannon. Our best efforts to focus her on postmortal recovery have been pretty basic: keep her away from the places she knew in her first life and convince her that this was not a good month to work on her tan. She dismisses any suggestion that she needed to attend nightly meetings of a 12-step support group with a regal flick of her head and a declaration that she didn't have time to waste on *tea parties with old biddies.*

The principal biddy in question was locked in a staring contest with Esmee when I made it through the door.

"Rosetta, I see you remember Esmerelda," I said.

Rosetta, our chairspook, leading grammarian, advisor on sensible fashions and sponsor for all spooks of a feminine disposition, greeted Esmee with a nod.

Esmee replied with a quick, "Charmed, I'm sure," as she scanned the room. "Where are the tables?"

"We use seats here, dear," Rosetta said. "Why don't you make yourself comfortable and I'll explain things after the meeting."

Esmee gave her a sly smile. "After the meeting, huh? Whatever you call it, duckie, that's okay with me. So long as I get to hear the gentle tinkle of those chips."

"Quite," Rosetta asserted.

Rosetta had more to say. In fact, I'm sure she had a lot of wisdom, advice and straight-forward orders for Esmee, now that Esmee had finally stooped to join her brother and sister spooks for mutual support on the long journey toward transcendence, fixing the problems or learning the lessons she'd overlooked during her first life.

Rosetta exchanged a meaningful glance with Cal, and whatever righteous lecture had been building up in her since Esmee showed her face this evening vanished like tissue paper down a toilet.

Cal was my sponsor, and he'd made an art out of communicating with the fewest words and slightest gestures. For getting Esmee into her first meeting, he twitched an approving eyebrow in my direction. Most meetings, he avoids eye contact and stares at the floor with his arms crossed over his chest, and when someone like me tries to take the conversation down a path that Cal doesn't think we ought to go, he lets me know in a way that's quick and unambiguous, although I'm baffled afterwards about what he did that carried that message.

Tonight I saw his eyes flicker to one side in a way that told Rosetta we ought not to expect too much too soon from Esmerelda. Or, as one of our program's many cliches puts it, *Die and let die.*

"Welcome to this meeting of the St. Sears group of Specters Anonymous." Rosetta took her place in the center of a circle of gray metal chairs. "Is anyone here in her first thirty years of recovery?"

She glanced at Esmerelda.

Esmee wiggled her toes.

"Anyone at all?" Rosetta added.

Esmee squirmed and fought to suppress a grin. She was here for the card game after the meeting, and not even Rosetta could deflate her enthusiasm.

Cal adjusted his crossed arms over his chest. Rosetta read the message in those subtle movements and shifted to the next item on her agenda.

"For our leader tonight, I've asked a new friend to talk about what our official literature calls the *perplexities, tremors and fantasies* that brought her to our recovery group. I give you Mary Beth."

Mary Beth was one of the wall huggers I knew from a few meetings, a newbie who stayed far away from everyone else, eyes wide with the fear that someone might notice her or *(shudder)* expect her to say something. Newbies aren't into communication, they're into panic.

Tonight, Mary Beth took a place with the old-timers in the innermost ring of gray metal chairs. She appeared to be young and earnest, and her bangs hung over her forehead and the tips of her ears poked through her brunette hair.

"Hello, family, my name is Mary Beth." Her voice picked up confidence with each syllable. "I'm a spook. And I'm honored to have the chance to tell you about my recovery."

"Hi, Mary Beth," came from most of the spooks in the room.

"Welcome, dear," Mrs. Hannity chimed.

"Yo, there," Hank said.

"Whatever," Gilda added.

Mary Beth had a nervous smile. "This is the first meeting I've been asked to lead. I hope I do alright."

"Hush now," Rosetta raised her hand in a stop-right-there gesture.

"Did I say something wrong?" Mary Beth asked.

Rosetta didn't answer. Attention focused on the basement wall, she could've been a basset hound tracking a squirrel across the yard, her eyes moving slowly along the wall to the door.

Every spook in the room followed Rosetta's gaze. Make that *every spook except one.* Gilda, ensconced in her black leather jacket, chains, purple fingernails and lips, and day-glow makeup, was the lone holdout who didn't seem to wonder who was about to join the gathering. Even in the afterlife, one expects a Goth to maintain high standards for indifference.

Mary Beth was about to jump out of her ectoplasm. "What? What?"

What floated through the door in a single file were three cloudy figures. Picture a trio of fog banks hugging three vague silhouettes. Sooty in color, more gray-ish than gray, like ashes that had sat undisturbed for months in a fireplace and were liable to disappear with the slightest wind, drifting into the room on clouds of silence.

(Note for readers: You've heard about electric silences? This was the analog version: no hissing to set your hair on end, but your hair had no trouble standing on end by itself.)

One after the other, the three silent, ashen figures drifted between the folding chairs to the center of the room and formed an arc in front of Rosetta.

Esmee jiggled an elbow into my spectral ribs. "You should have told me sooner they had plays at these shindigs. I wouldn't've fought you off."

"This isn't a show," I whispered back. "These are the Somber Sisters."

"What are they somber about?"

"Everything that isn't somber."

Her elbow was back in my ribs, and this time I was convinced she'd probe until she found my backbone. "They're putting us on, right?"

"The only things they ever put on are their personal storm clouds and, if you look real hard, you can see right through them."

"And your point is?"

"They have an utter lack of commitment to putting on anything. Even their own astral essence."

Esmee gave me a hard look, as though my explanation wasn't the essence of pith and clarity; then she leaned over her chair to peer under the cloud that enveloped the nearest figure.

Rosetta, who was rumored to be the secret author of the spectral hit, *1001 Ways to Start a Conversation with a Corpse*, had to show everyone that three spooks inches from her knees were no impediment to a nice chat.

"Our friends from the Somber Sisters are most welcome," she said. "Please feel free to make yourselves comfortable and join the discussion. I'm assuming that doesn't violate the rules of your order. Pardon me, I meant to say, *your disorder.*"

The three figures didn't move, nor did they say a word, neither flinching nor squirming, as though their presence was a sufficient rebuke to the rest of us who needed to share our tales of *trudging the road to a happy nap time*, according to one of our program's zippier sayings.

I believe that's exactly the point the Somber Sisters wanted to make. They are traditionalists. To their way of thinking, only insecure, wild-eyed radicals need to gather every night to swap stories and encourage each other in postmortal recovery. If the Uber-Spirit wanted us to hold nightly meetings, He / She / It wouldn't have stuck us alone in holes in the ground.

"Let's continue with our meeting, dear," Rosetta told Mary Beth.

"Sure." Mary Beth tucked in her chin, determined not to be intimidated by three silent ash-covered specters of unknown intentions and unproven powers drifting squarely in the middle of the room. "Here are the high points of my recovery."

The Somber Sisters repositioned themselves in an arc around Mary Beth, and continued saying and doing nothing.

Mary Beth took — what passes in the afterlife for — a deep breath and said, "I died. I came here. Who wants to share next?"

(Further note: We were talking about analog silences a moment ago. This next quiet moment was even more basic. Call it a pre-industrial silence.)

Esmee was the first spook to stir.

"I am ever so grateful I came here tonight." Her eyelashes flashed at the Somber Sisters like butterflies in a gale. "I was getting the depression that this place had a dress code. Surely, that's the only explanation for my ill treatment at the rehearsal."

"A rehearsal? There really is theater here!" This from a newbie in the back row in a baseball cap and sunglasses.

"Not the sort of acting that met my standards during my days trodding the footlights," Esmee said, haughtily. "But, I would imagine it's interesting for those growing bored with puppet shows."

"Puppets!" said a spook on the other side of the room, who for reason beyond my curiosity, had her astral hair in curlers. "I didn't know we had puppets."

Despite the presence of the Somber Sisters, the conversation followed its own careening logic until, shortly before halftime, Fast Eddie regaled us again with a tale about how he died with Plato's *Republic* on his mind, impressing only those few spooks in the room who (A) weren't thoroughly bored by everything Fast Eddie had to say, (B) knew enough about Plato to be intrigued by the yarn, and (C) didn't already know Fast Eddie qualified for membership in Specters Anonymous after a book fell on his head in the library.

Which ought to be a warning to philosophy majors everywhere.

CHAPTER

alftime is a tradition in 12-step programs. A pause comes to the discussion, a donation basket circles the room, and participants wander off to refill coffee mugs or light cigarettes or grab a few moments of tranquility on the outside steps.

Only the last option is practical for those of us on the spectral plane. I left my seat and gave a wide berth to the Somber Sisters who were still arrayed around Mary Beth's knees.

Hank was behind me. "Don't let it get around, Ralph, but those three critters creep me out. How can anyone go through the hereafter so glum?"

"Some folks think death is about lying still and being quiet."

"If that's what they want to do, good luck to them."

"Those fanatics are determined to discourage everyone else from doing anything else, except lying still and being quiet."

Hank shook his head. "I'd feel better if they'd scream from time to time. Then I could scream back. But I can't fight 'em if they don't come out swinging."

"That's their point." I examined the night sky that spread over us like a pink umbrella. "If they do anything – even if they just discourage others from taking action – then they're violating their own beliefs."

"I can't see anyone we know getting in line to join that outfit," Hank said.

"No way," I agreed.

The Somber Sisters drifted toward the door, still wrapped in their ashes and a kind of silence that can only be described as – pardon the rough language here – deadly. Off to intimidate another recovery meeting into inactivity and silence. But something had changed.

"Weren't there three sisters?" I asked.

"Absolutely." Hank pointed at each foggy figure as it passed. "There's number one. Number two. Number three. Number . . . ah . . . four."

Unmistakably four, gliding across the lawn in search of spooks with more animation than the Sisters' brand of orthodoxy allowed. They were identical in size, silence and gray ambience, although the last one in line had a saucy sway that set her apart from the others.

"They recruited one of our spooks?" Hank stammered.

"Esmerelda," Gilda said, coming up behind us.

Hank gave me a toodle-oo wriggle of his fingers and took off after the Somber Sisters, clearly convinced a night with them was more fun than a chat with Gilda the Goth.

I probably would have joined my friend if Gilda hadn't asked, oh so offhandedly, as though the thought just fluttered into her mind, "How's the homework coming?"

"It's coming along nicely," I said. "Just fine."

Gilda gave me a skeptical squint.

Homework, on my side of the daisies, is an all-encompassing word for those chores that spooks have to accomplish before we can leave this sidetrack on the road to forever, such as some first-life lesson we slept through or wreckage whose cleanup we should have scheduled before our funerals.

"I don't see how you can be so cool," she said. "If the key to my transcendence was sitting on a disc in a friend's computer, I'd be all over it like zombies in a funeral parlor."

My chin rose to a noble angle. "I don't want to inconvenience anyone. You'll understand when you've been in recovery as long as I have."

"But all you have to do is watch the DVD of an old TV show." Gilda's eyes widened like a startled raccoon. "And you have how much to look at? Didn't you tell me a month ago you were on the last disc?"

"Sure thing," I said, heading down the steps to the meeting.

Gilda snagged my arm. "Wait. That's not right. You didn't just say it was the last *disc*. Wasn't it the last *episode*?"

"Yeah. I forgot that too. The last episode. That's what it was."

My left leg was drifting through the door when Gilda pulled me outside. "No, I'm still not remembering this right. It was the last minute. You distinctly told me there was a minute left."

I gave it my sincerest shrug. "Look, we all make mistakes. When I said a minute I really meant – "

The chains on Gilda's leather jacket jingled; in fact, I thought they were about to go for my throat. Her fingernails clenched. She was a spectral lioness, shaking herself awake with a cranky attitude.

"You mean it's less than a minute?" she said. "Fewer than sixty seconds? Then you're out of here?"

"Something like that."

"How much like that? Be specific, Ralph."

I glanced at the place on my wrist where I once wore a watch. "I'd love to chat, but we don't want to miss the second half of the meeting."

MARY BETH'S EYES followed me into the room. Great. Now the newbie was going to team up with Gilda and chastise me for not seeing the rest of that DVD. Mary Beth kept smiling, and eventually I couldn't resist smiling back.

Hormones aren't supposed to have a place in the hereafter, but, let's face it, some of us have an appeal that can't be hidden by six feet of dirt and a chunk of marble. Call it my special burden.

Rosetta encouraged everyone to take a seat so we could start the second half of the meeting, and Mary Beth glided across the room toward me.

"I just heard you're handling the auditions for the play." Mary Beth's smile was so large I almost expected her bangs to rearrange themselves to accommodate it. "I had a little experience with the theater in my last life. I hope it's not too late for a tryout."

After Esmee's performance tonight, I wasn't sure seeing any spook emerge from an empty porridge bowl had much entertainment value. But Mary Beth had a spook-next-door kind of appeal, and I had a responsibility to my public.

"I'd be happy to give you a few minutes," I said, "although we're not doing formal auditions."

"That's okay. I'm not a formal actress." Mary Beth's smile got larger. Halfway to her chair, she put herself in profile and, with a wrist pressed against her forehead, said in her best Richmond drawl, "I have always depended on the kindness of strangers."

When the meeting resumed, raised hands rippled through the newbies. A newcomer named Jock said the Somber Sisters made him "wonder if I really believed in transcendence."

Veronica, who's been taking hauteur to new levels in the afterlife, said the Somber Sisters led her to question her commitment to her own death, although she was convinced the sisters were heading in the wrong direction regarding fashion.

Someone asked, "Does anyone know if you can be both dead and a Buddhist?"

As the discussion swirled around the room, I sank into myself. Ever since getting my own headstone, I've felt the key to my path in the hereafter is *The Honeymooners*, an old Hollywood sitcom, with Ralph Kramden, the main character, as my model. Now, dozens of episodes later, I was no closer to knowing what I was supposed to learn in order to continue my transcendence on the spiritual plane.

Only seventeen seconds remained on the final episode of the last disc, and I'll admit to having a crazy idea that as the closing credits scrolled down the screen I'd find myself on some astral escalator, zooming out of Eternity's slum district.

Or was this strange notion, floating somewhere between where my ears had been, actually the sensation of being a bit unnerved – okay, somewhat flummoxed – let's make that, moderately terrified – that the TV series would end and all my problems would be solved and my afterlife would transform into an eternity full of peace, understanding and clean fingernails?

No more Cal to avoid, no Hank to keep up with, Rosetta to irritate, or Gilda to be baffled by.

Where's the fun in that?

Nearly a half hour later, I snapped out of my funk as Rosetta said, "We have a nice way of closing," and rose from her chair. We formed a circle, held hands and recited our Transcendence Prayer.

When I glanced up at the end of the prayer, instead of the usual roomful of bent heads, I was startled to find, here and there, eyes staring back at me and mouths spreading in smiles that were too wide, too happy or too cunning. One even mouthed, "I'm ready for my close-up, Mr. DeMille."

I was awash in a stream of . . . well . . . adoration.

"Yeah, he's the one," I heard a newbie whisper to another. Three more looked in my direction and turned away giggling.

Like I said, you can lead a hormone to the cemetery, but you can't . . .

An astral hand tapped my shoulder. *(Note to readers: Ectoplasm-upon-ectoplasm contact in the hereafter is similar to physical contact in the first life, the major difference being that only spooks' egos can be bruised.)* I spun around to see Gilda from the corner of my eye backing away, and Cal, my sponsor in recovery, directly behind me, his arms crossed over his chest, his gaze for once rising to the level of my face.

"It's been a while, Ralph," he said. "I'd like to find out how you're doing."

"Busy, busy, busy. Haven't had a minute to catch up with you. Hey, I haven't had a minute to catch up with myself."

"Yeah." Cal nodded gravely. "That's the thing about minutes. They can be real slippery."

"What I meant was – "

But Cal knew what I meant. And I knew that he knew. And he knew that I knew. And so on down the line.

Cal recrossed his arms. "I'm sure you're not letting your theater project interfere with your recovery."

"Absolutely not. I'm just using the time I have left on this afterlife – "

" – the very small amount of time" – Gilda cut in – "the teensy, infinitesimal, unmeasurable amount of time left for you – "

"Right," I said, deflectingly. "I want to transcend to the next level of existence in the true holiday spirit."

"Glad to hear it." Cal gave me a rare pat on the shoulder. "Good idea."

He drifted away to talk to the newbies, Gilda drifted nowhere, Veronica buttonholed Rosetta and Mrs. Hannity to find out if there was a karmic program for posthumous recovery, and I fought off the spiritual version of dizziness. My sponsor was actually passing up an opportunity to grill me about my activities. This didn't feel right. Did he think I was cured of all my postmortal problems? Or was he giving up on me?

I looked at Gilda. "When I mentioned *the time I have left*, was it clear that was just a figure of speech?" I said.

"Sure. Just like the phrase *Let's go see the rest of that DVD* is a figure of speech."

CHAPTER

ilda and I didn't have much to say to each other as we made our way over the business district. I was trying to come up with a way to avoid the approaching moment of truth, and Gilda should've known the hazards of giving me any excuse to slip away.

We settled on a quiet, shadowy sidewalk a couple blocks from Cary Street. *Psychic Advisor* flickered from a neon sign in a bay window where a string of Christmas lights twinkled around an ugly purple vase.

"Margie knows how to put her customers into the holiday mood," Gilda said in a rare show of approval.

"Good ol' Margie," I muttered.

Margie is what we call a *twofer*. She has dental bills, a shoebox full of old income tax records, a valid driver's license and three library books that are so overdue she's embarrassed to return them.

She also has a heartbeat. Yet she's seen specters for as long as she can remember, swapped tips about biscuit making with the ghosts of Jane Austin and Emily Dickinson, and listened to enough doggerel from Jingle Jim to convince even a fatalist that dying may not be worth the effort.

Margie owns a collection of DVDs from the 1950s television series *The Honeymooners*, a black-and-white sitcom that holds — I believe — the key to that first-life problem I'm supposed to deal with in my second life in order to find out if there's a third round.

I tried watching the DVDs through a process that involves shrinking myself to near-subatomic size and whirling around a DVD disc. Unfortunately, my memory isn't what it used to be, and I have trouble sorting through the disc's dots and keeping straight what goes where. It's easier if Margie points a zapper at the set to get the DVD spinning.

"I'd be happy to go with you when you look at that final disc," Gilda said when we reached the steps leading up to Margie's plain wood door.

"I'll keep it in mind," I said. As usual, I was being too subtle for Gilda. She followed me inside.

Margie's waiting room was half crammed with chrome-framed tables, orange plastic chairs and other nightmarish relics from the 1970s. The clientele was a mixture of college kids looking for laughs and older folks hoping to reach loved ones. And spooks. Dozens of spooks jostled and bickered in the empty half of the room where Margie's former business partner once kept her stuff.

"Something's wrong here." I scanned the jumble of glossy furniture, fidgety customers and restless spooks. "Something's missing. Or out of place. What could it be?"

Gilda surveyed the room. "I'd say it's the customers. There's too many of them. I've always thought of Margie's as a boutique, not a warehouse."

"Nah, that's not it." I looked at Gilda for an argument, but she was gone. Probably too many spooks here for her. I mean, what's the point of being a rogue spirit if death is a group activity?

"It's been like this for a week," said a timid voice that I recognized.

I leaned over the top of the garish purple vase in the window, hoping to catch a glimpse of one of the specters who, for a variety of reasons, none of them plausible even to spooks, were trapped in the vase's ceramic skin.

"What happened?" I asked the vase.

Somewhere inside the vase, a spook named Whiner sighed. Everything in the afterlife had failed to meet his expectations. "When Margie lost her partner, she also got rid of those wonderful Tiffany lamps. She replaced them with something from a machine shop."

"But you're stuck in the ceramics," I pointed out. "You don't have to worry about photons eroding your ectoplasm."

"But the noise of them hitting the vase keeps us up at all hours," Whiner said.

"As an all-powerful spectral entity, you should know how to end the constant *pitter-patter-PING*." This from the vase's second resident, whom I call Sniveler. He believes I'm a minor deity.

"As a matter of fact, I've been meaning to take another look at the laws of physics," I bluffed.

A sigh came from the vase that could've melted a glacier. Letitia was joining the discussion. "Gawd, don't you just love a divinity who knows how to take charge?"

If Whiner and Sniveler thought I was a god, Letitia thought I was astral putty, and that seemed to balance the books.

"I understand Dawkins had a little surprise for you at the theater tonight," she said.

"Dawkins?" I've heard that name recently, but for the death of me, I couldn't think of anyone — spook or Breather — named Dawkins.

"He's new in the neighborhood," she went on. "I heard he talked Fast Eddie into letting him pick the spook who'd pop out of the oatmeal bowl tonight. I also heard he picked Esmerelda."

"And you didn't stop him? Or warn me? How could a spook who once had a single working brain cell let anyone bring Esmee to that part of town?"

Somewhere in the purple murk of the interior, Letitia must've been giving me a chilly glare, for ice was clearly forming around the base.

"Sorry," I whispered.

"Not a single working brain cell?" Letitia had gone from honeysuckle sweet to kudzu sour. "Not the ghost of a brain cell? Not even the memory of a brain cell?"

"Don't get your ectoplasm in a knot. If there's anyone whose IQ has fallen into the minus numbers, it's me."

"Should Esmee drop by, I'll make sure she knows no one here is qualified to give her any advice."

A heavy wooden door slammed shut, and although it doesn't make sense, I'm sure the door was in the ugly purple vase.

BESIDES THE OBVIOUS tactlessness of putting Letitia's name into the same sentence with idiots, there was another reason I should've known the discussion was wandering close to a no-go zone.

Letitia, you see, was the ghost of a potter whose ashes had been mixed into clay by a former boyfriend and made into a vase. Once in the hereafter, her spirit stumbled upon the vase and, like most spooks who've found their burial plots, lost all interest in transcending out of there.

Whiner and Sniveler — here's where the idiots enter the story — decided to check out the vase and, in another one of those few, but vexing, rules of the afterlife, couldn't leave the vase once they entered it, the vase being Letitia's *ad hoc* grave and spooks being stuck forever in any stranger's final resting place they should wander into.

As my friend Big G is fond of saying, *Even in Forever, we can't take back a card after it's been dealt.*

Okay, so my conversation with Letitia could have gone better. Just a tad more support for her specterhood, a dollop of compassion for those entombed with morons and a smidgen less speculation about her mental processes – that might have done the trick.

But who was this newbie Dawkins, and why did he keep butting into my afterlife?

I barged out of the waiting room, steamed down the hall toward Margie's private apartment where the DVD recorder was kept, passed the beads that hung in glossy strings from the doorframe to the suite's second, now empty office, reached the room on the other side of the corridor where Margie met with her clients and wallowed to a halt.

Gilda emerged from the door.

"Where've you been?" I asked.

"In Margie's apartment. It's right behind me. I can take you there if you like."

"Why should I go there?"

"To watch an old DVD that I happened to see. It's very interesting."

Ever had the feeling that time stopped? When that happens on my side of the Great Divide, where everyone has a future of infinite duration, there's this ear-numbing clanging and shuddering and the squeal of locked gears.

I had to open my mouth. "What did you see on that DVD?"

"The last seventeen seconds of a sitcom."

"What happened in that sitcom?" I took a gulp that seemed like the thing to do although it accomplished nothing.

"Characters said things," she said. "Stuff happened. Then the DVD ended."

"And then?"

"And then, nothing. The series was over."

"There's always something after *then*."

"I came here."

"What else?"

Gilda checked her fingernails, the floor, the doorknob, the backs of her ectoplasmic eyelids.

"Nothing. That covers the major points," she said.

The gears of time were still stuck. An ice age or two might have formed, gouged paths through the continents and melted into the oceans before she added: "Why don't you see for yourself?"

"Because . . . because." Sometimes I don't know what I think until I say it. I squeezed my eyes, parted my lips, wriggled my tongue, and spat out the first syllables that reported for duty. "Because I'd be leaving something undone."

"What?"

The beads hanging from the door of the empty office in the middle of the hall picked up the reflections from the holiday lights in the waiting room and scattered multicolored dots across the ceiling, floor and walls.

"I forgot to wrap my present," I said.

"Could you possibly be more unclear?" Gilda said.

"Sure," I parried. "But there's this other thing I gotta take care of first."

Shooting a disdainful look toward the door to Margie's apartment at the end of the corridor, just letting it know that I wasn't intimidated, I hitched up my astral trousers and glided into the room where Margie met her clients.

EVEN SOMEONE IN postmortality can sense a drop in temperature in a tiny room. The only light came from a string of bulbs around the base of the fishbowl that Margie used instead of a crystal ball. This being the holiday season, the bulbs twinkled.

An elderly gent in a cardigan sweater occupied a chair, with Margie in the other one. The rest of the tiny room — and I mean all the space between the floor and the ceiling, between the four walls, and under the chairs and table — was filled with sufficient spooks to populate a respectable cemetery.

They wriggled and shrank and elongated to fit me in. The spooks, I'm talking about here. Margie and her customer were barely breathing as they focused on the fishbowl.

"What's going on?" I whispered to a spook whose knee tried to share space with my chin.

"Shhh," several dozen spooks answered.

Margie shot me a hostile glance. The old-timer shook his head gravely and said, "I just can't concentrate tonight."

"I'm having the same problem." Margie patted his hand. "You're too sensitive to psychic vibrations, and the spirits are very unruly this evening."

"Are not," said the spook whose knee was trying to rearrange my features.

"Not me," another answered.

"I've been as quiet as a dead mouse," a third offered.

"It was the new guy," added the spook with the knobby knee.

Margie held up her hands. "Come on, let's hold it down."

The elderly gent who couldn't hear the chatter from the room's noncorporeal inhabitants, looked puzzled. "If I talk more softly, I can't be sure what I'm saying."

"Not you," Margie snapped. "It's the – "

The gent peeked over the top of his glasses. "I believe you have a gift, Margie. But the more you talk about hocus pocus and spirits of the dead, the more I'm inclined to doubt you."

I relaxed, leaned into the spectral crowd and waited breathlessly to see how good ol' Margie would talk her way out of this one.

She pointed at the fishbowl. "It's that darned fish. I keep picking up its spiritual emanations. It's worried about what happened to all the friends it went to school with."

"And it thinks those fish are in some sort of afterlife?"

"Where else?"

I checked my feet, half expecting to find astral guppies flapping around the hardwood floor. A nervous titter passed through the spooks jammed around me. Specters who might have made a mastodon feel insecure were easing out through the walls. If fish started coming to the afterlife, wouldn't they smell a lot like . . . hmmm . . . dead fish?

The elderly gent stood and pulled his coat from the back of his chair, his eyes fixed on Margie. "You look like a nice young lady. You wouldn't take advantage of a senior citizen at Christmastime, would you?"

"Not even on Halloween," Margie said.

CHAPTER

*T*he old gent slipped into the hallway and softly closed the door behind him. Margie slumped in her chair. In the fishbowl, the little guy looked puzzled, as though it was wondering what just happened.

"Looks like a busy night," I said.

"Give me a swift kick the next time I complain about not having customers." She puffed her cheeks in mock exhaustion.

"Rotten time to lose your partner," I said.

"I'll survive."

(Note to readers: Breathers talk about the elephant in the middle of the room, *meaning someone or some problem on everyone's mind, although no one has the gumption to mention it. In my circle of friends, we have* the spook in the middle of the party, *an entity who serves many of the same purposes as the elephant, although spooks have a more flexible dress code.*

(Esmee, last seen leaving our meeting with the Somber Sisters, is the spook in the middle of my party. She's the spectral incarnation of Margie's former business partner Sophie, now known as Esmerelda, a name chosen from her once-favorite brand of apricot brandy, and a major aggravation on my part of the afterlife. Both of us [that's Margie and me] have to be careful what we tell each other about her [that's Esmerelda / Sophie] because any misstatement could carry dire consequences for us [that's the three of us finally gathered into one pronoun].)

Whether elephant or spook, Margie knew how to ignore the obvious by going directly to the inconsequential which, as often happens, was me.

"What's on your mind?" she asked.

I nodded toward the fishbowl. "Didn't your pet fish used to have a buddy in there?"

"The other little guy went to the great fishbowl in the sky."

Margie rubbed a fingerprint from the side of the bowl with her thumb. The bowl's lone occupant, encouraged by her example in tidying up the place, wriggled to the bottom of the bowl and nuzzled aside the gravel, no doubt looking for cigarette butts and candy wrappers.

"Do you think he noticed?" I inched closer to the fishbowl. "Did he wonder where his friend had gone?"

"We're not talking about fish or former business partners, are we?"

And for several minutes, time that I knew Margie, with anxious customers in the waiting room, could ill afford to waste on problems from another sphere of existence, she listened to my plan to thank my buddies for all the hoots and hauntings we've shared by bringing astral performers into the traditional local production of Dickens's *A Christmas Carol*.

"In all the time I've known you, you've never gone anywhere quietly," she finally said. "I'll admit, though, to being surprised by the play."

"Too subtle?"

"You're not the kind of guy who's interested in piggybacking your ideas on someone else's. I'd expect you to create your own play. Take charge, raise the bar, clear the field, create a new normal. Or, in your case, a new paranormal."

"You're making it sound easy," I said with sham exasperation. "Just getting one spook to pop out of a bowl at the right time, with the right dialogue, seems to be beyond anyone's ability. And you think I've got time to hammer out a new, original script?"

"Isn't Specters Anonymous supposed to be an *us* program? You're forgetting everyone's favorite dead writer." Margie gave a smile that made me sorry I was dead. "Edgar Allan Poe."

I would've thrown up my hands in resignation if, my luck being what it was, I wasn't concerned about my digits flying off to a more rational solar system.

Margie glanced at her wristwatch, shot me a winced smile, then headed for the door. "I know you're going to come up with the perfect decision. And while you're at it, could you discourage your spooky buddies from hanging around my place? I've got so many spirits chattering over my shoulders, I can't give my full attention to the paying customers."

"Consider it done."

BACK IN THE waiting room, I was pleased to see Gilda was gone, although the place still had enough spooks to populate a battlefield. How do you persuade dozens of specters not to hang around someplace they all want to be? I mean, other than by telling them they *have* to be there.

Phil Budahn

And therein lay the answer.

"This is your lucky night," I said, waving from the middle of a chrome-framed table Margie must have stolen from a dental office. "We're about to put these premises under quarantine. The Spectral Protection Agency has reports of freaky contaminants getting loose. A major violation of SPA standards."

"SPA?" said a spook who'd brought his bib overalls to the afterlife.

"Sounds important," another said. "Better sit up straight."

"In another couple minutes," I continued, "no one will be able to get in here. Of course, you won't be able to get out either. But you don't care about that. The point is, you get to stay here longer."

"How long will we be stuck here?" came a voice from the back of the astral crowd.

I shrugged. "A while."

"How long is *a while?*"

I looked at the world's ugliest vase on the window sill. "Sniveler, Whiner? How long have you guys been inside that vase?"

Sniveler, as usual, was the first to rise to the challenge. "I wouldn't dare to make the smallest calculation in the presence of the Great God Ralph. Who knows when the smallest gnat falls. Who sees the tiniest wrinkle in the space-time continuum. Whose ectoplasmic socks I am unworthy to sniff."

"How can you worry about socks at a time like this," Whiner fussed, deep inside the vase. "This place is a mess. Where are we supposed to put visitors? Could we get some time to work on seating arrangements? Badges with everyone's name would be a nice touch."

A great sucking sound nearly reached the auditory level as the waiting room emptied of spooks. I followed them outside and watched spirits streak across the starless sky. They may have lacked the style of the New Caledonia Precision Spectral Flying Team, but they made up for it with gusto.

In less than seven seconds, not an ectoplasmic glimmer disturbed the blackness above the city. The heating units of the business district hummed lullabies to the interstate highway whose traffic murmured back sleepy lyrics.

The magical aura was ruptured by a voice in the shadows that blended a pompous Richmond accent with a down-and-dirty Tidewater tempo.

"To have been. Or not to have been. That is the question," said the speaker from the darkness beneath the bay window.

"I didn't think you stooped to remember anything by Shakespeare," I said.

"Shakespeare? Was that his little ditty? I didn't know the old Bore of Avon composed a single line that succinct."

"What can I do for you, Mr. Poe?"

"No, the question, my earnest and somewhat benighted friend, is: What can I do for you?"

Edgar Allan Poe eased from the darkness. He was dressed in his customary black, which accentuated the few dollops of color about his person: the silver glint of his cane's handle, the glossy sheen of his ruffled shirt, his waxen complexion, the eyes that looked too haunted even for the afterlife.

I checked for evil-tempered birds perched on his shoulders. Ditto for the top of his head. It seemed safe to answer: "What have you got in mind? No, let me guess. You've come to talk about the last scene in *The Honeymooners*. You were a critic back in the day, right?"

"Honeymooners? Was that something else by this Shakespeare fellow?"

"Look, I'd love to stay all night and bandy crowbars with you, but I've got a million loose ends to tuck into place."

"Gay, volatile and giddy — is he not? / And little given to thinking."

Hearing the italics in his voice, I froze in midglide. Or maybe it was the sudden appearance of a black cape with crimson lining that now lounged across his shoulders.

Poe picked up on my hesitancy. "Ah, good for you. You recognize those verbal gems. Fruits from a neglected masterpiece of the American theater."

I saw where this was going. If Edgar A- was enthusiastic about anything in the English language, it could have flowed only from one quill.

"You wrote a play?" I queried. "I didn't know they had musical comedies in the 19th century."

Edgar A- smoothed the edges of his cape. *"Politian*, it was called. A tragedy about unrequited love, political corruption, out-of-wedlock birth, a suicide pact, a murder, an overdose, an execution — "

" — and a cast of thousands."

"Actually" — Was that a blush on Poe's sallow features? — "it has a three-person ensemble."

"How many acts?"

The blush grew stronger, taking on a definite glimmer. The cape disappeared. The tip of the poet's spectral cane poked a tuft of dried grass that slumped from a crack in the sidewalk.

"I . . . um . . . never got around to finishing it."

"But it would have been great," I said.

"A classic of the American theater, a triumph of the human spirit."

"And death," I added. "Bodies strewn like rag dolls across the stage."

A faraway glint lit up Edgar A-'s eyes. "My public can never get too many corpses."

After Poe presented more details about the plot of his abandoned play, deftly highlighting the ease with which he could transform the existing text from a historical, continental drama into a Yuletide American classic, I counterpunched. The only treatment due an unfinished masterpiece was its completion. His adoring fans were entitled to — nay, demanded — nothing less than the composition in its pristine totality to treasure forever. The structure was staring him in the face. Who could resist the appeal of an 1820s Kentucky love triangle?

It was guaranteed boffo box office.

"I can see it now." Edgar A-'s hand swept through the darkness to arrange the scene. "Lalage is alone in the garden. The moon limns the theater with saffron rays. Stage right, a rustle. A scurrying shadow. It is a . . . a . . ."

"Raven?" I offered.

"Ah, yes. When all else fails, bring in the bird."

Exit Poe, stage left.

CHAPTER

At that moment, I'd admit to liking Edgar Allan Poe. Who couldn't admire the old boy when he despecterized so eagerly that puffs of ectoplasm came from his ears. He had a mission, a calling, a challenge. He may be dead, but he wasn't down.

He stood for something. Believed in something. Woke up each evening in Happily-Ever-After and couldn't wait to race out and accomplish something. Even if it involved writing poetry that few would ever read about gods that even fewer have heard about.

Not that I'm envious of his gusto or measure myself against his focus. I was smarter, more sophisticated. I knew the score: That any spook who rushed into the twilight with a confident smile didn't know what he was up against.

A voice spoke from the shadows of a tree outside Margie's with an authority all its own.

"Next thing I know, you'll be offering that palooka your rhyming dictionary."

"How's it shaking, Big G?" I asked.

"You'll have to ask the suckers with the knees that are knocking together. They're the ones doing the shaking hereabouts."

"Ain't that the truth?"

Big G runs the Triple A, more formally known as the Ace Acme Afterlife Detective Agency. He's the spook with his hand on the pulse of the afterlife, such as it is. He has a fedora slanted over one eye, a rumpled trench coat and a cigar stub twitching like a bloodhound's nose.

How Big G smuggled a stogie into the hereafter is the source of endless speculation among my social connections, although I've never heard anyone bring up the issue with Big G himself, probably because the intrepid questioner would then be expected to ask if it's true that Big G's formal name was Gwendolyn.

Personally, I didn't die to put myself through that grief.

"Your old trench coat is right where you left it," Big G said. "By the front door at the Triple A. Mrs. Pellywanger put a vase with a little flower next to it."

"Who knew Mrs. Pelly was the sentimental type? A flower, you say?"

Big G worked his stogie to the other side of his mouth. "Yeah. Crab grass is a flower, ain't it?"

"It's the thought that counts."

The spectral detective studied the silhouette of a house on the other side of the street with an alertness that made me wonder if he expected it to make a sudden move.

"Speaking of thoughts," he said, "reliable informants tell me you've got this scheme for putting a few spooks into a Christmas play."

"Just an idea I've been tossing around. Think of our friends wandering into the old Byrd Theater for the traditional holiday show, and there on the stage, big as death, are specters working in Scrooge's counting house, strolling beside the urchins in the street, popping out of porridge bowls. Our buddies will see that and know they're part of the holiday."

Big G adjusted the brim of his fedora. "Won't they be surprised? They'll be mighty appreciative of the work you and Esmerelda have done."

"That's kind of you to say that." Then the echo of Big G's words elbowed the smile off my face. "Esmee? Why would they thank Esmee?"

"Now we're getting to the pointy end of the issue." Big G drew the collar of his astral trench coat tighter. Preparing for a vigorous exchange of opinions or a tornado or chasing a usual suspect down the nearest dark alley. "Esmerelda says you're working for her on this theater thing. You're supplying the connections and she's supplying the brains. So she says."

"But that's not . . . How can she . . . I mean . . ."

"That's what I thought." Big G nodded at the brick wall of Margie's home. "Go ahead, kid. Hit something."

I curled my spectral fingers into a fist. Made a cool-eyed appraisal of the crinkly brick surface. Took a solid stance. Then rammed my head into the wall. Past the bricks and the wood supports, into the cinder blocks and beyond the insulating foam, then into the pipes. The sewage pipes.

I wriggled my head around to clear my thoughts. There's nothing like a good sewage pipe to focus your priorities. I reemerged while Big G was rocking on his astral heels, hands thrust deep into the pockets of his trench coat, cigar stub bobbing understandingly.

"Okay now, kid?"

"I'll feel better once I get within range of Esmerelda to do serious damage."

"She'll thank you for it later," Big G said. "No one ever stayed properly dead without a firm hand around their neck."

"These newbies today are being coddled."

Big G raised his hand to the brim of his fedora. "If I didn't know better, I might feel sorry for little Esmerelda."

"But you do know better," I hastened to add.

BIG G HEADED at a Breather's pace for his office near the Jefferson Hotel as a ribbon of gray slipped onto the eastern horizon. Sunup was about an hour away, time for all good spooks to return to those special places where we can be guaranteed darkness during the daylight hours. We call those hideaways *buckets* because that's what a lot of them were. My bucket is an old coffeepot in a home on Libby Hill, on the far side of downtown.

I gotta be tough with Esmee, I told myself. As tough as Cal was with me during my first confusing nights in recovery.

Tough! The way Cal listened to me grumble and whine for hours. And he'd share the most embarrassing moments from his own early nights. Sticking with me while I set a new postmortal record for most screw ups by a newbie, most of the damage self-inflicted, all because I hadn't listened to Cal.

As I left the blinking neon sign in Margie's window and cruised above the trees toward the slowly awakening day, my determination to straighten out Esmee was getting shaky, and for some unaccountable reason, I also found myself thinking about *little-ism*. That's Specters Anonymous-talk for spooks who try so hard to prove they're just an ordinary, nothing-special, aw-shucks kind of spirit that they'll grind anyone who says anything to the contrary into ectoplasmic powder.

Was the play just a way to have fun in my last few nights in this region of spookdom? Or was it about making me look good? Why should it matter whether Esmee claims some of the credit?

Whenever another spook does something that bothers you, check your motives, Cal often warns. *Preferably, check them at the cemetery gate before you go farther.*

Glancing at pine trees below that shaded the front lawns for half a block, I saw three spectral figures drifting on the sidewalks, sometimes turning toward the recesses of a front door or bending to peer under cars parked along the curb.

These were the Colonel's troops, spectral soldiers on never-ending patrols to protect their former capital, and I found myself wondering if they hadn't found the perfect cure for little-ism. Even on this side of the Great Divide, they were diligent about their assignments, part of a team, taking pride in the group, not in their own more-humble-than-thou-and-damned-proud-of-it attitude.

I was thinking about our faithful spooks in uniform and Esmee and the play as I glided between the downtown skyscrapers. Here and there on the streets below, three- and four-spook clusters drifted from one patch of shadow to the next, sentinels who never retreated, not even when they were carried, feet first, into a funeral home.

As I angled my glide path downward over Libby Hill, I sailed by the statue of a rebel soldier on a column in a small park where the spooks in gray assembled. Sunlight bled into the east; the park was deserted by its customary assortment of specters who usually lay on the grass or gathered in small groups to refight battles that should have ended a century and a half ago, cleaning their weapons and taking questions from astral tour groups that tonight had to be satisfied with reading the plaques along the base of the column.

A lone figure in gray gazed down the southeastern slope of the hill. Even from a distance, I knew the creases on the Colonel's trousers were razor sharp, the beard neatly trimmed, and the gold braid along his cuffs and collar dulled from the smoke of cannon that fell silent long ago. His eyes, though, his eyes were alert for signs of his troops, his *boys*, and the enemy that pursued the Colonel and his army through the eternal darkness.

I waved at the Colonel. He dipped his chin in reply.

A block past the monument, I reached the sidewalk outside a gray duplex and nearly collided with a spook in the shadows of a small tree.

"Whoops," I said, swerving away. "I didn't see you standing there."

"My fault. I should have seen you coming behind my back."

Which was a little snarky for the hour before dawn. I paused to take the measure of my companion.

He was taller than me, his face made of sharp angles and flat surfaces, his uniform so covered with dirt it could've been worn by rebels or Yankees. The rifle slung over his shoulder with a fixed bayonet seemed to drift in and out of the spectral dimension, making me wonder if I was seeing it or just expecting it to be there.

"The Colonel's got you folks all over the city tonight," I said.

"Can't assume the bad guys will take time off for the holidays," he said.

Why not? I was on the verge of asking, although I shudder to wonder what it'd do to my reputation if word got out that I was showing signs of restraint.

This soldier, I sensed, was different. Put it down to the way his face might have been carved from granite. Or the rifle that couldn't decide whether or not it belonged in Happily-Ever-After. Or the creepy notion I couldn't shake that he'd been watching my house.

"It's bucket-time for all the Uber-Spirit's good entities," I said breezily. "Good night, Private . . . er . . ."

"Dawkins."

"Good night, Private Dawkins."

C H A P T E R

awkins! Dawkins! That no good, snoopy, play-meddling meddler," I hissed as I paced the living room from the television set by the fireplace to the Christmas tree in the corner. With each pass, glancing more ferociously out the window behind the sofa.

Dawkins had left the street.

"I knew something was wrong with him the moment I saw him. How could one of the Colonel's spooks be so dirty? And why would a rifle not be sure what dimension it was in? And what was that spook doing spying on my house?"

"Spying?" Gilda drifted in the middle of the arch leading to the dining room. "Maybe he was standing guard. Have you thought about that? Protecting you, not threatening you."

"You don't know what else this Dawkins has been up to."

I brimmed with indignation. I overflowed with it. I had so much indignation I could've scooped off a couple gallons and still be highly indignant.

Gilda wasn't impressed.

"You mean, the way he told Fast Eddie that he'd get a spook to come out of the bowl in that play?" she said. "How was he to know you had issues with Esmerelda? Or that Esmee's first-life was spent a few blocks from the theater?"

"Which brings us back to my original question. What was he doing outside this house?"

Gilda shrugged. Shrugs were her major form of expression, although this time she added, "Spooks happen."

I followed her into the dining room. The table held an artificial Christmas tree about two feet tall, surrounded by pine sprigs that filled the room with a tangy scent. Across one wall stretched three shelves of coffeepots, from the space-age and quirky to the ornamental or plain. They had drawn Gilda and me to this house like magnets a long time ago.

"I've still got a few questions about how it went." I struggled to keep my voice from sounding like Whiner's. "Back at Margie's, I mean. When you went into her apartment. Where she keeps her DVD player."

Gilda studied me. I was almost convinced she might perch on the tip of my nose to get a closer look.

"No, you've already had plenty of chances to ask." She drifted halfway to the Art Deco pot on the middle shelf. "And, in fact you did ask. Several times. But you ran into a problem."

I struggled to recall our conversation outside Margie's office about the last *Honeymooners* disc. "I don't remember anyone interrupting us."

"Interruptions weren't the problem. I was." Gilda darted toward me. "If you want to know what's on the final few seconds of that DVD, you're going to have to go to Margie's and look at it."

"But you do know, right? You could tell me if you wanted."

"GGGGRRRRAAAAHHHH," Gilda explained before leaving for her favorite coffeepot in a *poof.*

UNUSED COFFEEPOTS ARE perfect sanctuaries for spooks who need protection from sunshine and harsh lights. And when the coffeepots had been retired from daily service by a collector, it's the kind of experience you'll only get once you've died and gone to Richmond.

I drifted into the hobo coffeepot with the handle cut from a broomstick, and before settling into a nice, placid puddle of ectoplasm for the duration of the sunlight, I sorted through the conundrums vying for my attention and, as sometimes happens, I resorted to the wisdom of Specters Anonymous for guidance and comfort.

Last things last has always struck me as one of the program's useless pieces of wisdom, right up there with *Use no hooks, It's never too late to have a good night* and *Speed limit enforced by drones.* I mean, if you're looking at a series of five things to do, why do you need a 12-step program to tell you that the fifth thing you do will be the final one.

Last things last.

Yet, I may be too quick to be cynical. *(Note to readers: I know, I know. I can hear a chorus screaming,* It can't be true, Ralph. Say it ain't so. Not you. *But I'm big enough to admit that I'm not perfect. At least, this time.)* There is another way to squeeze an iota of meaning from this cliche. To wit: Final things endure. And what is good-bye but the final thing? It's a summation writ large. The thing that will last.

As I settled into a glob of ectoplasm in the bottom of my hobo coffeepot, I permitted myself a weary smile.

In pursing my *last thing* – my formal *bon voyage* to all my friends from the theater stage – I wasn't avoiding the final seconds of *The Honeymooners* DVD and the message it must carry that will change forever the direction and timing of my transcendence.

Nope. Not one bit. Never crossed my mind.

HOURS LATER, THE subtlest change in the darkness inside my coffeepot let me know that evening had arrived. The patter of photons against the tin sides eased, replaced by the murmur of voices in the living room where the family was watching television.

I'm not a great believer in extrasensory perception. After all, as a resident of the spectral plane, everything I've got is extrasensory. But this evening, as I pulled myself together, I knew my sanctuary on the dining room wall was being watched.

Private Dawkins was about to learn that even a corpse could push his luck too far.

Slipping through the back of my coffeepot, I passed into the wall, slid down until I reached the timbers that supported the floor, then made my way about fourteen feet along a joist before passing through several trusses and coming up slowly through the floor, then through a chair and then the dining room table before whipping myself into shape behind the little decorative Christmas tree on the table.

Gilda was waiting for me on the tabletop, one leg crossed over the other.

"Tell me you're going to put a stop to this," she said.

"I've got everything under control." Only one detail needed to be nailed down. "Ah, which *this* are we talking about?"

She tipped her forehead toward the coffeepot collection. I peeked around a tiny green bough to see the wall.

A mouse had climbed onto the shelves. I shook my head and tried again. Make that a clump of mud oozing slowly along a shelf until it hit a pot and poured up its side. Pretty neat trick. Even on the astral plane, we don't often see mud flowing up a perfectly vertical object.

"Stop trying to think what it ought to be," Gilda said. "Just tell me what you see."

"I see Mrs. Hannity. Let's make that mini-Mrs. Hannity. She's three or four inches tall, and she's crawling along the shelf in a brown robe. Her hair isn't white anymore but brown, and it hides most of her face."

"What's she doing now?"

"She's rubbing her head against her arm. That's strange. Her head is moving, but her arm isn't. Now, she's licking her elbow. There the head goes again, rubbing up and down across her arm."

"What does she remind you of?"

"A crazy spook hoping she picked up some chocolate syrup on the sleeve of her robe."

Gilda arched her eyebrows, and I realized she was learning to say as much with those eyebrows as she used to get with a shrug.

She looked at Mrs. Hannity and called, "Mrs. Hannity?"

Mini-Mrs. Hannity straightened on the shelf. Weary determination sparkled from her tiny eyes. Mrs. Hannity flung wide her arms wide and sang:

"MIDNIGHT. ALL ALONE — "

I waved my hands over my head. "Okay, I got it. That's my favorite song from my favorite Broadway play. But I'm not putting on a musical."

Faster than a hummingbird's heartbeat, mini-Mrs. Hannity went from the coffeepots on the shelf to the tippy-top of the Christmas tree on the table. She was humming "On the Good Ship Lollypop" and tap-dancing her little heart out, as it were, all the while her eyes peeked above her wire-rimmed granny glasses and stayed steady on me, cool, in control.

"Depth, Ralph," Mrs. Hannity said. "It's about depth and experience. How can you know what to expect from an actress if you don't know what she's capable of?"

The balls of her miniature feet brushed the point of the bulb, her arms flapped wide, her face was as quiet as a lawyer's conscience.

I looked to Gilda for support, but Gilda had turned inward. I wouldn't be surprised if she'd forgotten that Mrs. Hannity and I were there.

"What we're looking for," I began, cautiously, "is someone who can appear on the stage at specific times when no one's expecting it and stick to a script. All the while, showing some pizzazz."

Mrs. Hannity stopped in mid-cakewalk. "Pizzazz. Are you about to suggest I *put more life* into my performance? I didn't come to the spiritual plane to become lively."

She was gone (*poof*) while I was sorting through the dozens of things I was about to say that I'd regret.

Did everyone in the afterworld know about my plans for the holiday play? One glance at Gilda stifled that question and made me begin to miss Mrs. Hannity. Meanwhile, the afterlife's most orthodox Goth had passed the point of being quiet and was approaching pensive, not an easy task while clicking one's purple fingernails.

"Depth and experience," she repeated, softly. "When other spooks look at me, do they see my depth? Or am I just another pretty face in black leather and chains?"

I would've loved to answer those questions – with creativity, an ear for the resonating phrase, and astral feet that know how to take care of themselves and anything attached to them – but I'm already recognized as Mr. Insensitivity on two planes of existence and, given my dealings with Mrs. Hannity a moment ago, didn't need to defend my title.

"No spook ever comes close to you, kid," I said.

"One did."

"Who?" I asked, although I really wanted to know if that was ectoplasm sparkling in her eyes. Why should she be leaking from there?

"Darleen," she said.

"Darleen? Ms. Happy-About-Everything-And-Even-Happier-Now-That-You've-Asked-Her-About-It? The Pollyanna of the astral dimension? Who'll tell you the seven-nostriled Gnorglomilblanders from the Artoriam Nebulae have a wry sense of humor once you get to know them?"

I stared harder at Gilda, hoping it'd help me understand what she was really saying. Darleen? The most recent member of our Specters Anonymous group to transcend out of here to a dimension with better accoutrements?

Was our resident Goth saying she envied a spook who could find the silver lining under every headstone? Next thing you know, she'd try convincing me that I didn't know how the afterlife worked.

CHAPTER

Gilda was searching the carpet in the dining room for some greater meaning as I drifted into the living room. The entire family – mother, father, boy and dog – were watching the black-and-white images on the television where a windblown, wild-eyed character clung to the steel girders of a bridge above the roiling black waters of a river.

Petey, the beagle who ran this house, lifted her head from between her paws to acknowledge my arrival.

"What do you think, girl?" I asked the dog. "Do too many folks look for answers around their feet? Are they looking in the wrong direction?"

At the word *direction*, Petey cast a guarded glance at the Christmas tree in the corner. It didn't take a dog whisperer to know that Petey wasn't deceived by the twinkling lights, tinsel and tufts of cotton. That tree was on probation with Petey, and at the first hostile move, that tree was going to wish it'd stayed in somebody's forest.

Hank was waiting for me on the porch outside.

"Why didn't you come in?" I asked.

"Gilda still there?" he answered.

"Sure."

"Next question?"

"Nice night," I said, testingly.

The pigtail at the back of Hank's head nodded in agreement.

I settled down beside him, grateful that there was no sign of Dawkins. Hank was one of the few spooks I could count on not to bring up the subject of the last, unviewed segments of the *Honeymooners* disc in Margie's apartment. So, of course, I found myself struggling not to bring it up myself.

The porch light was off, the trees lining the block shielded us from the worst glare of the streetlights. From the windows of most houses a single electric candle glowed; a few Christmas trees were set squarely in front of other windows, sending colorful spangles into the night. Down the block came the muted melody of a holiday carol.

We watched as a spectral patrol made its way down the street, rifles at the ready, bayonets fixed, heads swinging from left to right as the spooks in uniform swept the area for danger.

"I've never seen the Colonel put out so many patrols," I said. "Not even the night we had half the Union troops on this side of Eternity attacking us."

"The usual crowd isn't up the street either." Hank jerked a thumb toward the Confederate memorial a block away.

"Want to give the boys in uniform the old *booga booga*? Just a little scare. Something to provide them with something to shoot at?"

Hank, for once, was going to be the mature member of the discussion. "I've got an idea where the Somber Sisters are hanging out these nights. If you want a little action, we can rescue Esmee."

I watched the patrol move down the street. They were too far away and too protected by shadows for me to tell whether Private Dawkins was with them. I couldn't picture that stern soldier moving at a crouch, not even while charging across an open field into a battery of cannon.

Hank led the way a few houses to the right, then down the sheer cliff face and around the bottomland of Gillies Creek to a pair of rusted steel doors set into the side of Church Hill.

"You're kidding," I said.

"Watch me," Hank said.

He slid through the doors, and I was left outside wondering what signs I'd missed that Hank had an extreme case of postmortal dementia. For every spook learns within minutes after arriving on the astral plane that we must avoid the graves of others. Spectral trespassers of another's grave are stuck there for the duration of the physical world, even if the burial site in question isn't a formal cemetery or urn.

Spooks not hampered like Hank by residual traces of testosterone — or free from the constraints of minimal intelligence, like Sniveler and Whiner — are careful about going into any physical objects that might have become ad hoc graves. And what was Richmond but one big cemetery?

Me? I'm above all that. My only concern is not wanting to give anyone the impression that Hank has more residual testosterone than I have.

Slipping into the rusty door, I proceeded a micron at a time, alert to anything that might be embedded in the steel until only a few atoms separated me from the surface of the door and I saw Hank drifting back and forth in a tunnel.

"Glad you could join me," he said.

"Nothing to it."

"Then let me clarify a few things." He pointed to the earthen sides of the tunnel. "Possible grave." Then to the ceiling. "Another possible grave." Then to a three-inch pipe driven into the dirt on the far wall. "Hollow pipe. Not a likely grave."

"As someone recently told me, *Next question?*" I said.

Faster than a nervous electron, Hank respecterized himself to the size of a matchstick and dove into the pipe. I followed.

Aside from a few dents where a teaspoon or two of water had collected, the pipe was free of debris, and we soon popped out of the tube in a cavern where a railroad engine had been carved into a dirt wall.

Not carved, as it turned out, for this was an actual railroad engine, three-quarters buried when the tunnel collapsed in the 1920s, killing workers whose bodies were never recovered. Hence the hill's status as a grave.

Rocks and dirt spilling to the ground, a few lengths of railroad tracks running nowhere, a broken pick, a pristine shovel leaning against the side of the engine, someone's long-forgotten thermos bottle – all littered the floor of the cavern.

But no Esmerelda.

"Nice plan," I told Hank.

"Nothing to it." He peered through the open window of the engine. "You can come up with the next plan."

"I'll have it faster than you can whistle your favorite funeral dirge." And for once, I wasn't bluffing.

I glided to the side of the cave opposite the railroad engine. A deposit of clay had created a smooth, pinkish patch on the earthen wall. I cupped my hands to my mouth.

"Esmee, are you in there? If you are, let me know. Don't be afraid. I'm not going to hurt you for taking credit for putting spooks into the play."

Somewhere in the cavern a handful of soil slid hissing down the wall, a pebble bounced off a railroad track.

"Is anyone else inside?" I asked the dirt wall. "Come on, guys. It's no good hiding. I know you're in there."

Hank poked his nose within inches of the clay. "What's the matter in there? Worm got your tongue?"

"Let's try a little psychicology," I whispered, nudging Hank aside, then to the wall I added: "Me and my buddy are the only spooks here. The Somber Sisters are out looking for anyone having fun. It's safe to talk to us."

"Hmm," the wall said.

As hmms go, this hmm was thoughtful. Not a question. Not said in anger or jest either, but pure rumination. The kind of hmm a chess master says who's planning to take an hour considering his next move. After a hundred years in this hill, those spooks weren't about to be panicked into anything rash.

Rash, however, was Hank's middle name. "Esmee, are you in there?" Ectoplasm was beginning to leak from his ears. "This shouldn't be difficult, Esmee. One *hmm* for yes, two *hmms* for no."

Hank gave me a wink and eased back from the wall. The wall, in turn, stood there with a sense of calm that can only be described as wall-like.

I crossed my arms, Cal-like, to see if it'd make me any smarter. How would the afterlife look if I woke up one morning inside a hill and the only company I had for a century, aside from the occasional ant or mushroom, were the Somber Sisters?

"I gotta tell my buddy Edgar Allan Poe about this place," I told Hank, trying out my own wink. "He's looking for a rehearsal hall for his new play. It's about these lesser Greek gods who all work in an accounting firm in the Midwest. In iambic pentameter, with lots of *forsooth's*, *egad's* and *Aunt Martha's bodkins*."

"I want to come back to Martha's bodkins in a minute," Hank said. "But you lost me when you called Edgar A- your buddy."

I raised a finger to my lips and nodded at the wall, but that was too subtle for Hank.

"What the Roth are you trying to say?" he asked.

Faster than a fidgety finch, I was on him. Best friend or not, spook or not, I was going to find a way to hurt him.

Hank never took his eye from the wall as I cranked back an ectoplasmic fist and took careful aim at his jaw. "Over there, Ralph. The arrow. What's with that?"

Glancing behind, I saw what Hank was talking about. The clay bulged in a familiar collection of straight lines and angles. It was, in fact, an arrow of clay that lay horizontally and pointed to one side.

I let go of Hank and scanned the cavern wall. "It's trying to tell us to look in that direction. Do you see anything unusual? On the floor or sticking from the sides? I'll try the ceiling."

The clay arrow began to pulse. I didn't appreciate the pressure.

"Did I mention the music?" I asked Hank with my best stage whisper. "Poe wants to transform a little ectoplasm into period instruments for his play. Who would have thought the old boy was also a composer?"

A line of arrows now appeared on the sides of the cavern, leading directly to the small pipe we used to enter. *Exit* appeared in flashing dirt letters above the pipe.

Hank shrugged. "What's that mean? They think we forgot the way out of this heap?"

I gave the wall my harshest look. "Poe says he's done an original composition for the play. It's with bugles, bass drums and bagpipes."

More earthen letters popped from the cave wall above the exit sign. The new message said: *She went this way.*

CHAPTER

Slick as greasy smoke, we scooted into the pipe, passed through the outside door and emerged without incident on the flat tidal plain at the base of the hill.

The incident was waiting for us outside.

Hank spun on me. "What were you trying to do to me in there?"

The pigtail at the back of his head pressed tightly against his neck, the way it gets when he's preparing to simplify things for an idiot, and it occurred to me that trying to give Hank a rough time in the cavern might not have been my best idea.

I asked, delayingly, "Whatever do you mean?"

"I'm thinking about how I found out where Esmee had been. And about how I took you there. Then, all you thought about was getting out."

"But that hill was a grave. There were spooks there who were telling us to get out."

"And that's a good reason to leave, is it?" The pigtail shifted into high alert. "You don't know who those spooks are or what their agenda is. But because they tell us to go, you want to leave. Is that really a good reason to leave?"

"Ah," I suggested.

"Want to know what I think? I think you think too much. Even when you're not thinking. Especially when you're not thinking about a spook you don't think much of."

With that — And what else could anyone possibly add? — Hank left for his next challenge. *Poof.*

"YOU HANDLED THAT nicely," a voice said from behind a bush. "I was wondering how I'd get you alone."

42

"That's me. Thinking all the time. Except for those times I'm not thinking."

"I think I understand."

Big G drifted through the bush. His fedora was tilted at a casual angle, the collar of his trench coat upturned, the cigar stub that lived in his mouth, relaxed but in a vigilant sort of way.

I was sure that once I started talking, a few syllables would roll off my tongue that explained why, despite all sorts of evidence to the contrary, things here were under control. Before I could start, Big G raised a hand and stopped me in early mewl.

A slight straightening of his astral spine warned me not to turn around too quickly. Slowly, I rotated on my heels.

Along the banks of Gillies Creek, which carried rain water to the river from the hills arcing around the city's southeastern edge, came five spooks in a tight knot, crouching, rifles and bayonets at the ready, heads turning like clockwork dolls as they scanned the terrain.

"The Colonel is sure cautious this holiday," I whispered as they slunk past. "We saw another patrol at the top of the hill a few minutes ago."

"Something's riding the wind these nights," Big G said, "and it's not naughty spooks who've lost most of their ectoplasm."

"Do you know what's going on?" I asked.

"Not yet."

Because Big G was a class act, he kept his voice low, his expression was – excuse the harsh language here – deadpanned. I couldn't imagine Big G hiding in the bushes and going *booga booga* even when he was a newbie. If any spook could get to the bottom of things, it was Big G. Still, I went bug-eyed peering through the darkness for signs of anything amiss.

Big G studied the tip of his cold stogie. "Want another surprise? A bigger one?"

I scanned the sloping green hills of Oakwood and Evergreen cemeteries and wondered when spectral tanks would come rattling over the crest.

"Earlier, I had to break up a screaming match," he continued. "It was between your buddy Esmee and the Somber Sisters."

"The Somber Sisters don't scream."

"Try telling that to Esmee. Or to the apartments along Tobacco Row. Those spooks were so loud they managed to break into the physical dimension. Some residents called the cops."

"The Somber Sisters," I muttered.

Who went through the afterlife in their own clouds of ectoplasmic ash. Who made a religion out of total detachment from the things of all worlds. Whom no one ever heard whispering, much less raising their voices in anger.

"What were they arguing about?" I asked.

"Esmee wanted to find out where the parties were. The Somber Sisters wanted her to be quiet and smell the lilies."

"Who won?"

"Do you really need to ask?"

Big G had managed to break up the squabble by directing Esmee to Harrison Street, where the action on fraternity row would be starting once the frat brothers wrapped up their mandatory 10-minute nightly study periods.

I snapped off a two-fingered salute to the hereafter's best detective. "I think I can take it from here."

Before I left, Big G said, "One more thing," and I drifted back to the ground.

Big G's cigar butt was nowhere in sight, a rare event in my experience. He slicked down the brim of his fedora. The collar of his trench coat had gotten taller. A tic opened for business under his left eye, and a funny expression slipped over his face. I thought he was trying to inhale his upper lip.

He said, "If she can take it, so can I. Play it, Sam, play *As Time Goes By*."

"Interesting," I said. "Let me sleep on it."

USUALLY I LIKE to get from every Point A to each Point B by gliding at treetop level at a pace that's not much faster than a strolling Sunshiner. What's the point of being in an afterlife without cell phones if you can't enjoy the peace and quiet?

But, usually on those astral forays, I don't have to worry about coming between two armies that carried their old grudges into the afterlife. As Cal was fond of pointing out, *The best plan is always the one you haven't made yet.* Or, in this case, in trying to avoid two armies, I blundered into a third.

Even before I reached frat row, I sensed a concentration of specters that was thick enough to make an atheist want to douse himself with holy water.

Fifty or sixty spooks stretched down the block in several directions from one particular frat house. Everyone had a costume. I saw enough Tin Men, Scarecrows and Cowardly Lions to staff a dozen revivals of *The Wizard of Oz*, sufficient waifs with smudgy cheeks and empty porridge bowls to populate three Dickens novels, plus countless Beetlejuices, Grim Reapers, Killer Pumpkins,

Killer Snowmen, Killer Hockey Players, Santa Clauses, Nutcrackers, Jokers and even – this being Richmond – a smattering of Edgar Allan Poes.

Fast Eddie sneered at me from behind a gunslinger's curling mustache. I almost didn't recognize Gilda near the front of the line without her Gothic leather and chains. Instead, she wore white astral socks and a clean apron over a white dress and held a clump of ectoplasmic violets.

"Who are you supposed to be?" I asked.

"Pollyanna, if you please," she said with a curtsy.

She eyed me, I eyed her, and she added, "You are within one careless syllable of having a very unpleasant night."

I wriggled a toe into the concrete sidewalk. "And everyone is here because – "

"Someone saw She-Who-Must-Not-Be-Disobeyed go inside. And the word got out that this is where you were holding your auditions."

Gazing at the white wooden columns, chipped rails and hand-lettered *Delta Tau Chi* sign hanging beside a burnt-out porch bulb, I said, "So much for my little theatrical surprise."

THE BROTHERS OF Delta Tau Chi like to think of themselves as Richmond's version of Animal House, although the sisters in the nearby sororities call it the Bug Jar. A desire to put some respectability into their Saturday nights led the frat brothers to sponsor this year's Christmas play at Carytown's Byrd Theater.

Still the traditions of the fraternity must be observed. After dragging Gilda inside, I followed a vapor trail of bad cigars through the first floor and down to the basement.

At a card table suitable for a casino, Esmee flitted from one player to the next, still unwilling to admit the harsh restrictions of spooks dealing with the physical world. She peered over shoulders and whispered advice that was never taken, leading her to slap the neck of another unwitting cardsharp who responded by pulling the collar of his T-shirt higher to ward off the draft.

"Get rid of the three and the seven," she told another player who, when asked by the dealer if he wanted more cards, shook his head.

"Coward," she huffed. "I am surrounded by weaklings and nincompoops."

"Why don't you get into the game yourself?" I asked.

Esmee swept a hand through the cards. "I know when to hold 'em. And when to fold 'em. But I can't seem to pick 'em up."

"Bummer," Gilda said.

Esmee planted her fists on her waist and glared at me as though I were responsible. I glared back: She wasn't going to distract me from telling her to stop taking credit for putting spooks into *A Christmas Carol*.

"You people don't know how to have fun, do you?" she said. "You're just as bad as those mummers from last night, the ones in sackcloth and ashes."

"Technically, we're not people," I answered.

"And technically you wouldn't know how to have a good time if you stumbled into a barrel of clowns."

Gilda slipped between the two of us. "Are you saying Ralph is dull?"

"Duller than dishwater."

Gilda wrapped an arm around Esmee. "I knew we were going to get along famously."

She led Esmee to a part of the basement where battered sofas held frat members stretched out in varying degrees of stupefaction. Esmee was quite taken with Gilda's Pollyanna costume and, for a few seconds, even tried a blue smock and apron for herself. Behind Esmee's back, Gilda gave me a thumbs-up sign. She'd keep Esmee out of places where a newbie had no business going, letting me get back to my play before I started thinking about the benefits of a drama-less transcendence.

Before leaving the frat house, however, I thought of one thing that would help Gilda keep Esmee preoccupied.

Outside I drifted along the line of costumed spooks. Fast Eddie, in his Old West garb, was the first to get my nod, and after that the rest came easy: I just pointed at anyone sporting a spectral six-shooter on a hip. Gliding past a spook-sized chipmunk, I heard a familiar voice say, "Are you getting too important for your old friends?"

"Now that you mention it, I probably am. But I'll stoop to bring you along anyway, Hank."

So Hank and his twitching wet nose joined the costumed gunslingers who followed me to the porch.

"That's not fair," someone shouted from the long line of spooks waiting to get in. "We were here before them. You're not giving the rest of us a chance."

The grumbling spread. Faster than you could spell *resentment*, the costumed line of spooks dissolved into an astral mob. They rushed the porch and soon stacked three- and four-spooks high on the front lawn. Time to unleash my tongue and hope it didn't end up digging my grave deeper.

"I'm sorry, but our director is going in a daring new direction. He wants to set the play in the Old West."

"That's stupid," a heckler added. "Everyone knows *A Christmas Carol* takes place two hundred years ago in London."

"Maybe next year, it'll be set in" – my eyes tore through the crowd – "a fantasy kingdom. Or a haunted house. Or a galaxy far, far away."

"What about the chipmunk? How's he figure into the Old West?"

"Wyatt Earp was his best friend."

Catcalls flew from the crowd, along with a few cats. I lifted my hands for quiet, and a tomato – not a spectral variety of tomato, you understand, but an actual, physical, red globby thing – whisked over my head.

Just when you think a situation can't get worse, someone invites the poltergeists.

CHAPTER *Ten*

The crowd outside was on the verge of rushing the frat house when I let everyone know that before tonight's auditions began, we'd have a Specters Anonymous meeting. And the subject was *thanks-a-bunch*, which in recovery-speak means an hour-long talk about how glad spooks are that they can't have a cup of coffee or chocolate chip cookies.

In no time, most of the spooks on the lawn recalled another commitment that'd slipped their minds, and when I asked the three remaining specters who'd like to lead tonight's discussion, each of the laggards came up with a reason to be elsewhere.

Which left me with one chipmunk and six or seven gunslingers to take into the frat house. In the basement we joined Gilda who'd managed to free a sofa in the corner by sitting down on — and eventually sinking into — the bellies of two slumbering frat boys.

Esmerelda, Hank and the other spooks took up positions midway between floor and ceiling around a card table that wasn't, in the strictest sense, there. Each player donated a trace of ectoplasm that Esmee converted into a deck of cards.

"Pity you don't have money or chips to give the game a little spice," I observed.

"This is poker," Esmee said. "Pity don't enter into it."

She held up a finger from which a gold droplet twinkled in the dim light. Ectoplasm. They would gamble with the precious, irreplaceable essence of spookhood.

"Those stakes are too high for me," I said.

After telling Esmee not to deal her in either, Gilda followed me up to the ground floor of the frat house where bicycles leaned against the foyer walls and aluminum beer kegs served as tables in the living room.

Gilda, still in Pollyanna mode, moved with a new lightness, her arms held from the sides of her astral body, her glance lowering to check the way her apron and dress seemed to flow, her feet in tiny blue slippers instead of spectral combat boots.

"You can go back to being a Goth now," I said.

"No, this is okay." But her voice had a trace of anxiety.

"It's lucky you wanted to be Pollyanna, just when" — I caught myself before finishing — *just when we had an opening for one.*

More was going on here than I'd noticed.

Darleen, the last spook from the St. Sears group to have the undisputed title of Miss Ever-Cheerful-&-Perky, was gone, and now Gilda had taken up her ribbons and apron.

Was her attitude going to follow? I was about to find out, for Johnny Spivey, the guy responsible for volunteering this fraternity to stage a holiday play, came behind Gilda, his arms wrapped around a cardboard box filled with paint cans, rolls of canvas and other props.

Conditions were ripe for an EVF encounter. That's *Ectoplasm Versus Flesh.*

Gothic Gilda would pay no more attention to a Breather passing through her than a spook would give to a gnat. On the other hand, a true Pollyanna would sooner leap into a tanning bed than have unseemly contact with a stranger's liver.

Two steps away and closing fast, Spivey bumped the handlebar of a bike, which rattled and clattered as it slid down the wall. Spivey lurched aside to avoid tripping over a wheel, Gilda turned toward the noise, and Breather and spook eased past each other with centimeters to spare.

We were back on the porch when another test came to me. I asked her, "How about coming with me to check out the rehearsal?"

To which a true Pollyanna would say: *What fun. How can I ever thank you for thinking of me?* While a Goth would reply: *When were you dropped on your head, Bozo?*

But Gilda said: "Yeah, whatever."

SO I ARRIVED at the Byrd Theater with Gilda in tow as the staff was locking up after the night's last movie and the frat guys began hauling scenery onto the stage from a rear door. The back row of the balcony was the best place for a couple observers from the astral plane. I settled into the darkest shadows, while Gilda drifted along the railing.

If I didn't know her better, I'd suspect she'd been dipping into embalming fluid somewhere. "Which is it?" I finally asked. "Are you a Goth or a Pollyanna?"

"Can't I be both?"

"You can, but you still have to make a choice. Are you an overly-optimistic Goth or Pollyanna with a dark side?"

"Dunno."

Yeah, Gilda could teach career politicians how to dodge a tough question.

The theater's screen rose, and the frat members began positioning the plywood replica of an outside door under the guidance of the director. The dapper man, still wearing a bright green sweater over his shoulders like a shawl, gave painfully precise instructions – "Six inches more to the right" and "Tilt the top seventeen degrees toward me"– before stomping onto the stage and doing everything himself.

"Perhaps I might offer some assistance." Edgar Allan Poe respecterized on the back of a chair in the next row.

"Have you finished adapting your old play for a Christmas pageant?"

"Gracious, no. The Muse is not summoned by the snap of one's fingers." Poe gazed at the ceiling as though the Muse in question had a summer cottage there. "I was referring to your present conundrum. It brings to mind a prank popular when I was a lad. We called it the Cross-Eyed Test."

"What are you talking about?"

Edgar A- hadn't become a literary legend by letting just anyone impede his narrative flow. He continued as though I hadn't said a word: "We enjoyed the usual boyish larks – wearing worms in our hair or putting live minnows in our mouths and spitting them on young ladies – the regular sort of hijinks."

"I can see it now," I muttered, my attention distracted by Gilda as she left the balcony for the shadows on the catwalks above the stage.

"At some period of our impressionable lives, for reasons that defy analysis now, the highest form of entertainment involved crossing our eyes."

"Yup."

"Our families warned us – and this must have involved some coordination among households, for we lads all seemed to have this revelation at the same instant – that if we weren't careful, we'd cross our eyes and they'd be stuck in that position forever."

"Hmm."

"Your friend Gilda reminds me of that story. Although, as a member of the opposing gender, she's coming upon that lesson backwards."

Like a sleeper awakening in a strange room, I tried to bring into focus the gloomy figure with weary, watchful eyes staring at me.

"Would you mind explaining that explanation?"

"Only if it were absolutely necessary."

Edgar A- twitched his ankles to examine his boots in the gray light, and I knew beyond a doubt that someone acquainted with all the gods and heroes of Greek and Roman mythology, down to Zeus's nephew's best friend's neighbor's cleaning lady, wasn't interested in bandying wits with me.

Against my better judgment, I tried again, "Please rephrase what you said about Gilda crossing her eyes backwards."

Poe floated over to my row. Planting his silver-handled cane between his legs, he leaned his chin on his hand and watched the director arrange the stage.

"Gilda's Gothic stance hasn't achieved anything for her," he finally said. "She wonders if a new image of herself would *take*. That, like crossed eyes, she'd find herself stuck as Pollyanna for a very long time."

"What are the odds of that happening?"

"As I always say, *If the apron fits, wear it.*"

"You always say that, huh?" I parried.

"Incessantly."

WHEN THE DIRECTOR switched his attention to a technician coming down a balcony aisle with a spotlight to mount on the railing, Gilda drifted back to the balcony from the catwalk over the stage.

To the long list of things I don't understand about Gilda, I should add her relationship with Poe. Like two cats, they make a leisurely study of each other whenever they're in the same room, circling slowly at first, sniffing and snuffling, then pointedly going their own way. Nothing that happens later can force them to acknowledge the other until the next encounter.

This routine made a sketchy sort of sense when Gilda was decked out in black leather and chains, and Edgar A- had the air of a 19th century mortician between clients. Who would still be standing when the final bell rang on the contest to be the afterlife's most dismal representative? But now, with Gilda determined to put a smile on her face, even if it involved lug-nuts and a soldering iron, she and Poe had dispensed with the circling ritual.

She went directly into not noticing him when she came up to me. "They're about to start the rehearsal. Who've you got to represent us spooks in this scene?"

"Hank is handling tryouts. Take it up with him."

"Hank's not here."

I scanned the auditorium below for spooks with the edgy bravado of actors waiting for an audition. "Since you're the only one who bothered to show up, why don't you give it a try?"

Put that suggestion down to force of habit: Just couldn't miss a chance to tweak Gilda. So wasn't I surprised when she pursed her lips, glanced at her shoes and gave what would pass in the normal world for a nod of agreement?

I gestured toward the stage. "Your adoring public awaits."

"What do I say?"

"Anything but *Boo*."

Gilda glided to the stage, and I could have sworn she looked as though her feelings were hurt.

"Did I say something wrong?" I asked Edgar A-.

"You were the essence of tact." He rolled his cane pensively between his spectral fingers. "If, that is, you were dealing with a Goth."

"But I'm dealing with a Pollyanna now," I finished. His point was that my snarky treatment would bruise a Pollyanna's delicate soul.

I leaned forward to watch Gilda descend into the shadows at the side of the stage. Would she worry about the wrinkles in her outfit if she were wearing her black leather jacket and leotards instead of a white dress under a blue apron? Had she ever held her hands behind her back and rocked on her heels like that?

"Okay, Ted," the director said, squinting in my direction, his voice projecting distinctly from the stage. "Let's see what we've got."

The searchlight on the balcony railing rattled like a box of empty tin cans, the technician flipped a switch, and a circle of greenish-gray light appeared on the mock door beside the director.

"Zero it in," the director called, and the circle of muted light zigzagged its way to the center of the door, aided by the director's efforts to grab the beam and shove it into place.

Once the circle of light settled upon the knocker, he said, "Cue Marley," and the lighting technician wriggled a sheet of plastic into the spotlight. Waves rippled over the lighted spot on the door as a face appeared in a grayish-green halo.

It was a man's face, drawn in thick black lines. The eyelids and jowls were heavy, the thin mouth unfit for any pleasant expression, and the tangles of hair that shot out from the sides and top seemed a natural byproduct of thoughts fermenting in a sick mind.

"There was nothing at all particular about the knocker on the door," the director declaimed. "Then let any man explain to me, if he can, how Scrooge saw in the knocker Marley's face."

Edgar A- leaned forward in his chair. "I think I know that fellow. I'm sure I saw him entombed somewhere."

"Your fans must all look alike after a while," I said.

On the stage, the director drew a finger across his own throat, the lighting technician clicked off the spotlight, workers scrambled to mark the door's position on the stage and Gilda made her theatrical debut.

Where Marley's face had been, Gilda's head now emerged, a bonnet tied beneath her chin with a wide ribbon. A spasm worked its way across her lips, and I knew I was witnessing Gilda's efforts to smile.

"Would anyone like a fresh cookie?" she asked.

CHAPTER

No sooner had Gilda uttered her single line of dialogue than the stage was rushed by a pack of spooks from the St. Sears meeting who must've been stacked up below the balcony to watch the performance.

"Brava, brava," said Rosetta.

"That was splendid," Mary Beth cooed.

"You rock girl," Mrs. Hannity said.

As carefully as a ballerina on her tiptoes, Gilda made her way around the director, curtsied prettily to the empty audience chairs and joined the spooks gathered in the aisle.

"Do you really think it was good?" she asked Mrs. Hannity. "I felt so silly."

The elderly spook wiped the ectoplasm behind her spectacles. "You were so convincing, I could cry. I'm sure I can smell cookies that'd just come from the oven."

That seemed to settle the question in Gilda's mind. Spooks tend to believe Mrs. Hannity because she reminds everyone of their grandmother. Even Cal and Rosetta, whom I'm willing to bet didn't have grandmothers.

Poe and I glided down beside Gilda. Until this moment, she'd been a postmortal legend for her insistence that she didn't need friends, but now surrounded by admirers, a puzzled smile glazed her face.

Rosetta praised her for her diction and a delivery that reached the highest seat in the balcony while still sounding conversational. Jingle Jim wanted to talk about a poem he felt inspired to compose. Fast Eddie offered himself as her agent.

"The sky's the limit, kid," Fast Eddie said.

Gilda looked at me. "What do you think, Ralph?"

"After that, no one else would dare to audition," I said.

Edgar A- lifted his astral cane, scratched himself behind an ear with the silver handle and shot me a guarded look. When a writer with Poe's professional resume gets cautious, I pay attention.

"Let's say that everyone else is a long shot," I added. "But they're entitled to a chance."

"Of course." Gilda was the essence of compassion. "I couldn't live with myself – or die with myself, or be dead with myself, or you know what I mean – if anyone was treated unfairly because of me."

"Aw," her fans said in chorus.

In the wave of goodwill and adoration that swept over the spooks by the stage, Cal caught my attention with a twitch of an eye. He wanted a private word away from the crowd.

Since my first nights in Forever, Cal has guided me away from the sunshine habit by the 12 steps of Specters Anonymous. He's been my conscience when my own notion of justice goes offline, my friend, my confessor, my drill sergeant and sometimes my nanny.

"I know you're busy with your play." He crossed his arms over his astral chest. "But I've got a quick question."

"Take all the time you need. What don't you understand?"

Cal didn't bat an eye. "Are you still interested in recovery? Do you want to work the 12 steps? Does transcendence mean anything to you?"

"Actually, that's three questions?"

"Then let me boil it down to one. What are you doing to help *the poor, still-suffering spook?*"

"Can we go back to the earlier questions?"

Before he could respond, I put my plans into terms that had the best chance for getting his approval, completely uninfluenced by the fact he was gliding a couple feet away and staring at the carpet with such intensity that I expected the molecules in the floor to scoot out of the way and create a sinkhole.

My pitch went like this: "Seventeen seconds after I begin watching the end of *The Honeymooners* disc, I'll know the great lesson that's been blocking my transcendence, and I'll be out of here for the next destination on that long, winding, astral road. The play is my two-hour *Adios, Sayonara, Auf Wiedersehen, Bien Par* and *Later Bro* to the spooks who've traveled with me this far on the second dimension."

"So it's about you," Cal summarized.

"You've been around me too long," I rebutted. "No, I want to show everyone that spooks can have holidays too. That the next time Breathers put on *A Christmas Carol*, my brethren and sistren will remember that someone once made the astral plane an important part of the play. That if I can do it, so can they."

"Getting you out of here isn't enough of a gift?" Cal said.

"It's a legacy. Marking the trail for those who follow. Giving a positive example of death in action."

"And this is going to help them because – "

"We're putting the spirits back into Christmas. And, this time it's going to stick, by Jiminy."

I swatted the air for emphasis, grateful that my mouth had talked me out of trouble while my brain was still examining the angles. I wished I could've summoned the New Caledonia Precision Spectral Flying Team for pyrotechnics.

The spooks fussing around Gilda went silent as they waited for Cal's reply. Even the director paused on the stage, gripped by an intuition he couldn't explain that something monumental was about to happen.

Cal looked up from the floor. "Who's Jiminy?"

BEING IN A windowless theater, we might have prattled about Gilda's spectacular performance until the retirees arrived for tomorrow's lunchtime matinee if Fast Eddie hadn't said he needed to double-check that the basement room on Church Hill was ready for tonight's meeting of the St. Sears group.

Hank went to Gilda, extended an elbow and asked if he could escort her to the meeting. A few of my sistren spooks were clearly miffed when Gilda took his arm, but most watched with politely envious smiles as Hank and Gilda drifted through the lobby doors.

"Aren't they a sweet couple?" Mary Beth said.

"So long as you don't wonder what their bones are doing now," Roger added.

Veronica, who's lately been trying to get in touch with her Zen-self, looked at Roger with a disapproving, "Oommm."

There's nothing like a postmortal realist to take the zing out of the evening. Still most of the spooks gliding out of the theater looked content, so I wasn't surprised to see that some had traded a smidgen of ectoplasm for a sprig of holly or an astral replica of a snowball.

I was close to falling into a holiday mood – at great danger to myself and those around me – when Jingle Jim tapped my arm.

"Perhaps I may offer, if it doesn't seem bold, / My talents for scripting the tale you want told. / The best stimulation for the holiday spirit / Are thoughts that are rhyming, or comfortably near it."

"You want to diddle with the script?"

"It may sound pointless, it may sound crazy / But I prefer to call it, gilding the daisy."

I searched the balcony for Edgar A-. "You realize that another writer might have strong feelings about this."

"Whomever might that be?"

"Yeah, who?" I echoed, throwing up my hands.

It was a fateful gesture. For my spectral head tilted backward as my fingers reached for the heavens, and I was looking at the catwalks high above the stage. The reflected glow from the footlights projected slabs of darkness upon the theater ceiling, creating a phantasmagoria of bitter light and honed shadows upon the face that glowered down me.

"Private Dawkins," I whispered.

The theater reacted to my revelation with a *crack* so powerful it was felt in the hereafter. Spooks filing into the lobby sprang through the ceiling, sconces along the walls rattled, the upturned bottoms of the audience seats flopped open in dismay, and two stagehands walking away from the mock door used for the Marley scene dove for the side curtains.

Wood chips were raining on the stage as the director rushed back. "Is everyone okay? Are we missing anyone? Who's got tonight's sign-in sheet? I want to see that sheet now, people."

But I didn't need an accounting. Or a written explanation. One of the spotlights above the stage had broken loose and landed on Marley's door, reducing the cheap prop to fragments and dusty fibers. Nor did I need fingerprints to know who to blame. For the spotlight started its downward trajectory from the exact spot overhead where Dawkins had been standing.

Cal rushed to the stage as the director nudged a large piece of the wreckage with a toe.

"What happened?" Cal asked.

"Some spook found a way to unfasten a light," I said.

"Why would anyone do that? The door didn't look that bad."

"Maybe they didn't like the actors."

I looked at him. He looked at me.

"Besides Gilda," he said, "which of our friends have been on that stage lately?"

"Only Esmee. But that was last night."

Cal drifted downward until his eyes were level with the stage, and I knew the tradesman's instincts that had followed him into the astral plane made him eager to examine the rubble.

"I'll stick with Gilda," he said. "You track down Esmee."

We left the theater and came out above the marquee. The glow from the streetlights sent an unpleasant tingly feeling through my ectoplasm. Like dogs warning a rival, the engines of the passing cars growled softly. Coeds were looking in the front window of a bookstore across the street, their voices as soft as a glass wind chime.

"Might we be overreacting?" I asked, although I was stunned to be the one asking that question. Me, the most freewheeling spirit in the cemetery.

"A dropped spotlight isn't going to hurt one of our spooks," Cal said. "But the spook who dropped that spotlight . . . who knows the damage he can do to himself? Might even try to hurt one of our friends."

"'Nuff said."

We parted ways after we left Carytown, with Cal proceeding over the downtown area to our Church Hill meeting, and me heading down to frat row, where I last saw Esmee.

THE LORE OF the afterlife doesn't have many instances of spooks harming each other. Excepting the occasional spook who found his own grave and discovered an interloper in his casket. We also have spooks who've been nursing grievances since the days they had hormones. Then there are the ones convinced that they – and only they – truly understand the rules for postmortality. And the poor souls who have to deal with those who have all the answers.

Okay, so the more I tried to convince myself the hereafter was a safe place, the more I realized I'd be better off in another solar system.

A patrol of Civil War vets inched along fraternity row as I arrived on Harrison Street. I would've asked if they'd seen a spook matching Esmee's description, but the Colonel doesn't like having his troops distracted from their duties, so I made my way through the foyer of the frat house and passed a meeting of the respiring crowd underway in the living room.

Although meetings aren't in my plans for the afterlife, someone in the room used the phrase, "our play," and others answered with a chorus of groans, and I had to find out what was going on.

Johnny Spivey had taken up one end of a sofa. His dark hair had his trademark part in the middle of his head, and paint had splattered his hands,

T-shirt and blue jeans. Spivey was one of the stars of the art department on campus. We go back a ways. It makes sense that he'd be involved in his frat house's production of *A Christmas Carol*: the backdrops showing a Victorian-era accounting house and snow-covered London streets were done by someone who knew how to handle a paint brush.

"That's not going to work," Spivey was saying, and because you can't always rely on verbal communication in a frat house, he shook his head and wagged his finger for emphasis. "Each of the three ghosts of Christmas needs his own backdrop. Then we'll need one for Scrooge's bedroom, another for his office and – "

" – and there goes our budget for costumes and the theater rental." This from the only guy in the room with a sport coat and a pipe peeking from a breast pocket. Let me guess: This was the frat president.

"What's more important for a play than the setting?" Spivey said. "That's where we should be putting our money. Give the audience a better experience."

The president eyed the other guys in the room, gauging their support. "There is that other irksome little expense we keep ignoring."

Spivey slapped his hands against his legs. I could tell his manly restraint was being tested to the limit as he added, derisively, "Liability insurance! What could possibly go wrong on that stage that would hurt anyone?"

"Oh, boy," I muttered to myself.

CHAPTER

smerelda hadn't moved since I left her in the basement earlier in the evening. Still squatting midway between ceiling and floor, accompanied by six spooks in cowboy garb around a card table that only existed in a purely spectral sense, still studying the ectoplasmic cards in her hand.

"Who's ahead?" I whispered, sidling beside her.

"NO ONE." The answer came from Esmee and every spook in the game.

My jaw dropped in amazement. "Frat boys interested in liability insurance. Now a game of poker in a seven-way tie. Will wonders ever cease?"

A couple of cardsharks moved their hands closer to their astral six-shooters. Esmee gave me a look that'd strip the paint off one of Spivey's backdrops in seconds.

"They're mulling their opening bids," Esmee said.

A single golden drop of ectoplasm sparkled from the tip of her finger. Glancing at the other players, I saw that no one else had gone that far toward risking the smallest dab of the precious essence that distinguishes a spook from an empty place in the cosmos.

"This is probably a bad time to mention that our meeting will be starting soon," I said.

"'Twarn't nothing bad about that," a gunslinger next to Esmee said, tossing down his cards.

"Nope," replied another. "Don't want to miss a roomful of spooks talking about how glad they are to be dead."

"Ain't a proper night without remembering to say, *Thanks-a-bunch* for being here," said a third.

I looked at Esmee. As if I needed a tiebreaker.

She was scooping up the cards and flicking a few gleaming droplets to each player as she converted the deck back into ectoplasm. "The cowards didn't have a chance against me. One of them got a look at my hand and knew he was done for."

"What did you have?"

"The two and three of diamonds."

"That explains it."

I angled her towards the steps leading up to the foyer but she managed to miss the stairs and drifted through the cinder block wall. I looked at Roger. "Shouldn't one of us go in after her?"

"Be my guest," he said. "But I warn you: Esmee took a break from the cards a few hours ago, and when she came back, she was her old self."

"Clueless, conniving and controlling?"

"I'm thinking of something farther back. Before she decided to spread confusion through our neighborhood."

In her pre-posthumous existence, Esmee had a fondness for all things alcoholic, a weakness that shouldn't have any effect on her behavior on the quiet side of the Great Divide. How's a spook to get tipsy when we can neither eat, drink nor inhale anything that rattles our senses. Heck, we don't even have senses.

But, of course, I can always be wrong.

About this time, Esmee emerged from the basement wall and stared at me as though I was the spook who needed explaining. "Weren't we acquired before we came here?" she said. "Lemme try that again. Didn't I meet you before we met?"

Uh-oh. This was sounding familiar. In a mooshy, well lubricated, beginning-to-fall-to-pieces sort of way.

"Naw," I said. "I would have remembered you."

"Would've, could've, should've. I'm saying I do remember you. What do you think about that?"

"Maybe you're remembering a nightmare."

Esmee rested her chin on my shoulder. She tried to get her eyelashes to beat faster. "It was more like a dream."

One of the frat guys who'd been watching the TV in the basement passed through us while I was thinking of something clever to say. The liver. I'm sure it was the liver that glopped through my nose. Don't you find yourself wishing that livers would mind their own business?

"Hey, I'm drifting here," Esmee said to the guy's retreating back. "Can't you see I'm drifting here?"

"Actually, he can't," I offered.

"Ear-elephant," she said, which under the circumstances was close enough to *irrelevant*.

I followed her up the stairs to the ground floor, glad that she had stopped trying to remember that we first met when she had a heartbeat and she worked as a psychic with Margie, although most of her time was spent on quality-control tests for the domestic producers of apricot brandy.

When we reached the living room, the frat's entertainment committee was discussing the financial crisis facing their stage production, and the presence of so much testosterone in a confined space knocked her further off-kilter. Soon she was sitting on the fraternity president's lap with her spectral eyebrows inches from his bobbing larynx, sometimes squinting, sometimes cocking her head from one side to the other.

"I don't believe we've been formally intruded," she said, waggling a finger through his nose. "But you can't fool me. You're a naughty boy. I can tell."

The president rubbed his nostrils with the back of a hand. A chill had drifted into the room. Or so he thought.

Spivey got to his feet, all smiles.

"Where're you going?" the frat president asked.

"Gotta get to work," Spivey said. "More backdrops to finish now that we're not going to waste money on insurance."

"You can't leave." Esmee drifted up from the president's lap. "I haven't started with you yet."

Spivey was unaware of the new admirer trailing inches from his back. Esmee's infatuation lasted until they reached the foyer, when a couple of frat members came from the basement, each swinging a pack of beers in one hand and a bourbon bottle in the other. They charged up the stairs to the second floor, with Esmee in hot pursuit.

I stayed in the living room as the meeting broke up, listening to the participants chat about the play and other issues that involved the fraternity, until I was sure they hadn't learned about tonight's accident with the spotlight crushing the mock door.

Drifting upstairs to retrieve Esmee, I followed the music and raucous laughter but she wasn't at the most likely gatherings. I glided through the walls on both sides of the second floor hallway, then the third, and finally the fourth floor, until I reached a room with a bed that'd been properly made. Shelves over the desk held display cases with mounted butterflies and glass containers smoky with chemicals. From one of these jars poked a pair of miniature spectral legs. I grabbed a foot and pulled.

Esmee's eyes rolled in her head when she popped out, making complete flips in her sockets; her tongue didn't fit in her mouth anymore, and her fingers clawed at the shelf to pull herself back into the jar. Her being astral and the shelf being physical, the only thing she accomplished was to push her hand through the wood.

"Just a few more minutes, Mom," Esmee whined. "I'll get up if you let me sleep for a couple more minutes."

I didn't need to check the label on the jar to know Esmee had found the embalming fluid. *Being dead isn't the worst thing that can happen to a spook,* Cal likes to tell newbies. *That distinction belongs to spooks who are dead and stupid.*

Want to know what *stupid* looks like in the hereafter? Try to picture me gliding out of that frat house with a balloon tied to a string. Then erase the balloon and the string and insert Esmee, Esmee's leg and my fingers gripping her foot. That'll give you a picture of me escorting Esmee home. Don't ask which one of us was stupid.

Snow had begun to fall, dusting the lawns with white powder and sending silver chutes through the headlight beams of the few cars on the road. The night was quiet and solemn, and I might even have called it magical if Esmee weren't singing *A Hundred Bottles of Beer in the Wall.*

As we passed the Confederate memorial with its obelisk, I saw the Colonel pacing alone on the edge of the hill, a commander who carried into Eternity his responsibilities for his troops.

Speaking of responsibility, the Colonel and I needed to have a chat.

I took Esmee through the dining room wall of the duplex at the end of the street. The lights were off, except for the Christmas tree in the corner of the living room, which sent little shards of red, gold and green ricocheting throughout the downstairs. Pretty to look at, even for a spook, still the tiny lights put out enough photons to give the most enthusiastic holiday spook the heebie-jeebies.

Usually when we have guests of a spectral nature, I let them pick their own coffeepot from the collection on the wall. Esmee was too busy introducing herself to the pine cones on the dining room table to handle any decisions. I shoved her into a ceramic kettle with a Currier & Ives landscape etched on the sides, told her that if she dared to move before sunset there'd be no holiday gifts for her, and scooted back to the Confederate memorial.

The wind had picked up, sending cottony drapes ruffling along the hilltop; the lights from homes across the river twinkled through the flakes. Without the usual collection of spooks in gray uniforms lolling around the obelisk, practicing their rifle drills or sharing war stories with astral tourists, the little park seemed huge. I settled next to the Colonel.

"That was nice of you to give your troops time off for the holidays," I said.

"My boys have had nothing but time for more than a century." The Colonel's Southern accent was genteel, his voice calm, his commitment to civility unshakable. "I can't say I've heard anyone ask for more of it."

I gestured toward the empty park. "Then where is everyone?"

"On patrol."

"What's going on?"

The Colonel eyed me coolly. "If I could answer that question with any confidence, I wouldn't have put all my boys on patrol."

I eyed him back, just as coolly. It lasted less than three seconds. I tried another approach.

"I have the greatest respect for your outfit. I've never said a single negative word about any of our boys in gray."

"However – "

The Colonel let the word hang in the quiet air like a blimp that could either float away or explode in my face, and suddenly I wasn't interested in waiting for myself to come to the point.

"I had a run-in with one of your soldiers. A Private Dawkins."

"What was the nature of this encounter?"

Oh, boy. The nice thing about not being taken seriously is that I don't have to be picky about choosing my words. No one is ever paying attention. On the downside – and this moment was on the cusp of a very long downward plummet – I'm unprepared for any situation that calls for language that hits a specific point, saying no more and no less than what's intended. I'm used to flinging my adjectives and verbs in the general area of what I'm thinking and hoping for the best.

"I was at the theater tonight. I think one of your soldiers made a spotlight fall onto the stage. He could have hurt someone."

The Colonel pursed his lips, his eyes crinkled, trying to focus on something through the flurries.

"Overlooking for the moment the difficulties of one of our kind unfastening any physical object," he said carefully, "we're left with the problem of the intended target."

"Gotcha." I replied so quickly it was awkward to add: "Um, what was the problem with the target?"

"A spook who was discharged from the physical dimension at least a hundred years ago wouldn't have a grievance with anyone there now."

"Maybe he has a grievance with a spook."

The Colonel's expression was midway between sad and puzzled. "Odd weapon, then, to choose. A falling spotlight. Which will have no effect upon one of ours. What did you say this spook's name was?"

"Dawkins. Private Dawkins."

He turned back to study the storm. "I know all my boys. Dawkins isn't one of them."

Thirteen
CHAPTER

*Y*ou can push a battlefield commander only so far, and after the third attempt to find out why the Colonel was sure that Private Dawkins wasn't in his outfit, I had reached that point. I said good-bye before the Colonel offered me an armed escort out of the park.

Halfway to my favorite restaurant where my friends would be gathering in honor of the seasonal peppermint ice cream soda, the storm intensified. Sheets of whiteness hid both the familiar lights of Shockoe Bottom ahead and the towering black obelisk behind. I stopped beside the railroad station's clock tower to consider what made me think I was accomplishing anything. Why should I need a legacy? Plenty of spooks had passed this way before, and I wasn't aware that any had left a record of their passage.

Esmee would or would not find her way through the afterlife without me. Gilda would keep up her Pollyanna persona or revert to being a Goth or she'd find another path. Margie would get her business back on a solid footing or she'd move on. Cal, Hank, Big G and the rest of my buddies would still be dead if I weren't here.

What's to stop me from going back to Margie's, shrinking myself to a size that could read a DVD, then to absorb the great lesson that delayed my transcendence and move on to whatever comes after the afterlife?

I glanced back at the obelisk on Libby Hill. A gust of wind parted the snowy curtain and I saw the Colonel on his lonely vigil. Did he really believe that the war he'd carried beyond the grave could be won or lost? Or was it enough that he was looking after his troops, his boys?

As was usual for this hour, spooks and Breathers shared the booths in the River City Diner. The Breathers were mostly engaged in conversations over late night sandwiches and coffee, while the spooks congregated at the tables that had cakes, pies, cookies or sweet drinks. Every spook seemed to have his own theory about how to get enough of something to register on whatever replaced taste buds on the astral dimension. Most of those theories involved sneaking up upon an unsuspecting crumb.

I'd barely passed through the door when I realized something was wrong. Granted, the Sunshiners kept glancing at the front window to watch the snow slanting down to the sidewalk. No, it was the spooks who were behaving oddly. Not a single resident of my side of the Great Divide was talking. Nor, for that matter, were they hunched over the desserts on the table, as befits entities worshipping any concoction with sugar or chocolate. Not this roomful of spooks. They drifted silently at their tables and booths with ramrod postures, eyelids lowered and heads angled so I saw the sides of their faces.

If I didn't know better, I'd've guessed I was interrupting a funeral oration.

Fast Eddie shared the booth nearest the door with a middle-aged couple. I slid to the bench opposite him.

"What gives with our friends?" I asked.

"Is something wrong?" Fast Eddie answered, not quite catching my eye, his among the many astral heads turned to show me their best profiles. "I was just thinking," he said. "*STELLA, STELLA!*"

"Ah, so that's it. Word's out about the play, and everyone wants a part."

Fast Eddie seemed offended, a notion I would have thought impossible scant seconds ago. He said, "Wouldn't you? I mean, if you weren't you? Or for that matter, even if you stayed you, maybe you'd too."

"?"

"*Stella, Stella.*" This time he was whispering. "*My baby doll's left me. I want my baby.*"

A cell phone wriggled and ratted on the table in front of a woman who was picking her way through a salad. She looked at the phone, shook her head, then went back to her salad. From the phone, visible only to residents of the astral plane, a scowling green face erupted.

"How about having that guy submit a digital video and letting him move on?" the cell phone-sized entity said. "It's getting so, a working spook can't concentrate. I ask you, how many bytes per second can you supervise with someone yelling, *Stella, Stella*, in your ear?"

Perhaps this is a good time to talk about wraiths. They're spooks who've chosen to spend their afterlives in cell phones, computer tablets, digital watches, electronic calendars and other small electronic devices. Opinions are divided whether wraiths are still trying to understand those contraptions or whether they're continuing a battle over first-life grievances.

Wraiths are small, green and obsessive. They're all named Spunky. Not to be confused with their cousins who inhabit laptops, personal computers, servers and mainframes, who are all called Sparky.

"Give a spook a break, buddy," said Fast Eddie.

"Breaks are what you get from playing with sledge hammers. I don't deal in breaks."

Fast Eddie gave Spunky a third-degree stare. I could practically hear the ectoplasm sizzle, the cell phone began to wobble and Fast Eddie, whose talent for manipulating physical objects earned him the title of *Tosser*, was about to let everyone in the diner – wraiths, spooks, Breathers and tweenies – know that he was unhappy.

At the cell phone's first rattle, the woman reached for the device. As her hand came down, Spunky scooted into the screen. Fast Eddie had a triumphant smile.

"That'll show the little imp," Fast Eddie said. With a nod to me, he rose from the bench and added, "You know how to reach me if you're interested. Just remember this: *Stella, Stella.*"

Fast Eddie went over to join Roger at a table on the second level, and I was relieved to see that most of the spooks had turned their attention to the desserts in front of them. I was no longer facing a roomful of profiles.

With one exception. Spunky respecterized out of the cell phone after the woman set it down. "Here's one more thing to remember: Christmas isn't Christmas without the holiday wraiths."

"Actually, it's pronounced *wreaths.*"

"Wreaths, wraiths, wroths. I don't care how you say it," Spunky said. "Just remember us."

"'Natch."

Rosetta was heading toward me from a table in the back, her eyes glittery. She had the tight-lipped grin of a spook who needed to share with me a favorite passage or two from the classics, something from *Ralph's Death for Dummies* or *1001 Great Obituaries.*

Spunky got my attention by tapping my spectral wrist with his little green ectoplasmic finger.

"*Luke, I am your FAH-THUR,*" he said.

With a wink, he dipped back into his cell phone, leaving me to struggle for a moment with the image of Spunky wielding a light-saber in a death-or-death struggle with the forces of darkness. To think of the wraith losing was only slightly less probable than having the little guy win. Wraiths have dedicated their afterlives to taking another byte out of the Apple, as it were, and even Darth Vader wouldn't have the gumption to stand up to them.

"I am sorry you missed our meeting tonight," Rosetta told me, smoothing down her sensible skirt as she settled beside me. "I understand you had other responsibilities to attend to."

She had the wariness of a spook ever anxious about my language, especially my creative synonyms for friends on the astral plane, chief among which are *roadkill, cemetery fodder* and *maggot-bait.*

"My night is incomplete until I hear your sweet voice," I answered.

That pushed the needle on her wariness meter farther into the red zone.

"A most interesting spook led tonight's meeting." Rosetta spoke carefully to examine each word for lurking *entendres*, double or otherwise. "He asked me to pass along his greetings to you. He was one of our veterans. I'm sure you'll agree that we don't see enough of them at our gatherings."

"I'm sorry I missed him," I said.

"Private Dawkins promised to return for our next meeting."

"You said Private – "

" – Dawkins." Rosetta came close to making an unspectral sigh. "A very intense spook. I saw great depths in him. Not the sort of gentlespook I'd expect to make your acquaintance."

Force of habit kept me from reacting to Rosetta's news while I grappled with the implications of having Private Dawkins cross my path again. There was something about the sharp angles and smooth surfaces of Dawkins's face that made me wonder if stone statues had finally been admitted to the hereafter.

Making sense of the past was a major duty in the afterlife for me and my buddies, and hadn't some statues seen enough of the past to tax a supercomputer? And what about those supercomputers, huh? Shouldn't *artificial intelligence* be entitled to an artificial afterlife? And if intelligence becomes a factor in posthumous placement, how far down the waiting list will the rest of us clowns be shoved?

In no time, I'd thought myself into such a jumble of confusion that I was barely aware of Rosetta leading me from the restaurant by the hand, down Main Street and into a courtyard with high brick walls and shadowy corridors where Edgar Allan Poe was perched on the roof of a building that formed one side of the quadrangle and Rosetta moved to the portico on another side where she allowed one spook at a time to glide before me and talk for about a minute, then Hank escorted the spook through a door with a *Gift Shop* sign.

I was in the courtyard of the Poe museum. That's what I finally came to understand. The snowfall had dwindled to sputtering flakes. Wide slashes of ground at the base of two courtyard walls were free of snow, while the rest of the lawn had a thin veil of white laid on top of the withered grass.

A spook I didn't recognize was stretched out on the air in front of me, singing about the dream she'd dreamed in a death gone by. Rosetta consulted a spectral clipboard in the shadows of a door overlooking the parking lot and a bustling crowd of spooks. Hank tapped a foot next to me, not so much keeping the rhythm as counting the seconds remaining in the singer's audition.

I caught Edgar A-'s eye and exchanged squints with the poet, barely aware that Hank had already thanked the singer and led her to the gift shop door, while Rosetta brought another hopeful before me, read a name from her clipboard that I didn't hear, and slid back to the shadowy corridor while a young spook in a blue uniform stuck his thumbs in his belt and began:

"Four score and seven years ago — "

And I found myself studying the young vet, making sure this wasn't Private Dawkins outfitted in clever camouflage. If those weren't Dawkins's eyes, then what did Dawkins's eyes look like? His mouth? His nose? And what was that indefinable rigidness about Dawkins's posture that managed to look both relaxed and tense at the same time?

Before I knew it, I heard the soldier say, "Shall not perish from the earth," and his fist punched the air as though the very molecules were resisting his message.

Hank mumbled his thanks to the orator, Rosetta glided forward with the next candidate, and Poe came down from the roof.

"You are quite sure this ordeal is necessary?" he said. "Give me another night or two, and you'll have five acts in blank verse that will make Milton weep and Christopher Marlowe break out in hives."

"Then it would be your legacy," I mumbled.

"What's wrong with that?"

I didn't answer. Edgar A- wouldn't understand. Besides, Rosetta had brought in the next candidate for the audition: a spook decked out in an outfit suitable for any character from Dickens who started singing that tomorrow was only a night away.

CHAPTER

Fourteen

he sun was sneaking below the eastern horizon when Rosetta suggested we call it a night and resume the auditions after sunset, although a line of specters still stretched across the parking lot of the Poe museum.

"I'm hoping those spooks will leave," she told me. "They're terrified about someone taking their place in line."

She was joking, of course, but not really.

Hank hitched up his astral trousers. "I'll let them know I found a nice, safe, dark barrel. We can hold an all-day meeting if anyone wants to hang around. That'll get their attention."

As a pink blur spread overhead, the photon level in the courtyard was high enough to make me antsy. But from the shaking heads in the parking lot as Hank talked to the group, I could tell some spooks waiting for their auditions were reluctant to go to safe places for the daylight hours.

"Why would anyone put themselves through this for a few moments on stage?" I said to myself.

Rosetta heard. "Maybe for some, this is *their* legacy."

GILDA WAS WAITING for me in the dining room of our duplex on Libby Hill. I was finished with auditions and legacies, done with figuring out Dawkins, and most emphatically *finis* with any spook who came to me with expectations of a posthumous stage career, a song in their hearts, a dance in their toes or Georgia on their minds.

Gilda wore her black leather jacket and chains over a white Pollyanna dress and apron. One eye was layered in mascara and eyeliner, the other untouched; her lower lip was purple, her upper lip a posthumous gray.

"I'm so happy that you invited your new friend to spend the day with us," she said. "So very, very happy."

It took me a second to get on the same planet as Gilda. "That's Esmee. I brought her here because I didn't know where else to send her. I hope you don't mind."

"Why should I mind? I'm enjoying that song she can't stop singing. Such a cute little melody. But I might enjoy it even more – and I hope I'm not asking too much here or showing my insensitive side – if you could choke her until she stops."

"I guess your legendary unflappable sense of calm has been duly flapped," I said.

"Flapped, flopped, fizzled and frayed."

"And you expect me to do something about it?"

"In a word, *Yes.*"

Gilda had now gone entirely Goth: snow-white complexion, all lips and nails purple, enough mascara on each eye to hide the Colonel's regiment, black leather jacket crossed with chains that were taking an interest in the conversation.

"Do you need more information?" she added.

"I think we've covered the essentials," I parried.

A spook who stumbles upon embalming fluid is like a non-swimmer who falls into a vat of whiskey: they're convinced the only way out is to keep swallowing. Suggestions from strangers aren't helpful, I knew from unpleasant experience, an insight that pointed my nose in the right direction.

I drifted to the upper shelf where Esmee's antique coffeepot sat. "You know, Esmerelda, your singing has a special admirer."

"Really?" Esmee answered from inside the pot. "It's nice to know there are classy spooks who 'preciate classy class. *Thirty-eight bottles of beer in the wall, thirty-eight bottles of beer. You take one down –* "

"Your new fan used to be a voice coach. She has some pointers for improving your act. One pro to another pro."

"Improvements?" Esmee's voice got smaller, tentative. "A coach, you say?"

"Why don't you sleep on it? We can talk about this in the evening?"

The coffeepot gave the tiniest wiggle, and I wasn't sure whether that was Esmee nodding or despecterizing into a puddle of sulking ectoplasm.

Gilda returned to her full Pollyanna regalia, without a trace of her Gothic roots as she dove into the spout of her favorite coffeepot with an odd pucker on her lips. Even Pollyanna needed time to perfect that Pollyanna grin.

I liquefied into an ectoplasmic puddle before I reached the bottom of the hobo coffeepot that protected me from the daylight. Not even a ripple of discontent stirred the surface of my slumbering self as the planet took another slow pirouette, photons blasted the earth, the long day waned, the slow moon climbed and, one-by-one, bottles of beer left the wall like smoke drifting on a breeze.

HOURS LATER, AS I struggled to consciousness, someone was calling attendance.

"Suzy, Jim, Tinkerbell."

Tinkerbell? Was the afterlife dropping all standards?

I pulled myself together next to the dining room table. The gray glow of twilight was yielding to the cool, steady presence of night. In the kitchen, Mother rattled her way through the routines of washing the dishes. From the living room, where the lights from the Christmas tree sprayed multicolored dots on the walls, came the voice of her young son.

"Clarabell, Annabell, Dawkins."

I shot into the living room.

James William lay on his belly on the sofa. His chin rested on the upholstered arm, while a finger brushed against the pine needles. On the floor was the beagle Petey, her own chin tucked between her paws.

"Who is Dawkins?" Mother called from the kitchen.

"He's a soldier." James William nudged the three-inch plastic figure in desert fatigues that hung from a bough.

I've never had any luck as a people-whisperer and don't know how to develop those skills now, but there's only one way to find out if I've recently found the knack.

"Where did you get that name?" I asked, positioning myself beside James William's left ear. "Did you meet someone named Dawkins?"

James William acted as if I wasn't there, not an unreasonable position from his spot in the universe. I, however, although a long-time resident of the astral dimension, was becoming thoroughly miffed by being ignored by a child. A pipsqueak. A mere prospective future member of Specters Anonymous.

I inched closer to James William and spoke louder and slower. "Dawkins. Have you met him? What did he look like? Was he real or a Christmas tree ornament?"

"Aw, you're trying to reach out to a Brick. Isn't that sweet." This from Gilda who'd respecterized on the back of the sofa in Pollyanna form. "Have you ever heard anyone say that Breathers were Bricks? I have, and I think it's terribly clever."

"Almost as clever as spooks who have to change their appearance a couple times a night," I answered.

If I was getting under Gilda's ectoplasm, she did a good job hiding it. She smiled and drifted off like a tourist who'd never seen twinkling lights and mistletoe before, taking in the nativity scene on the window sill, the foam snow sprayed on the glass, greeting cards lined along the mantle like trophies, and faux evergreen sprigs on the TV table.

Gilda, I thought, needed to get back to basics. "You're dead. You don't have to pretend to be anything."

"Does that mean I don't have to learn some great lesson and transcend?"

"Well . . . sure you do . . . but . . . ah —"

I was starting to miss the old Gilda. The one who came after me with a verbal club. Not the one who'll creep up on an unsuspecting friend with an incisive question.

"How does your sham Pollyanna fit into real change?" I asked.

"Sham it until you am it," she answered sweetly.

It sounded like a nugget from Specters Anonymous, but not one I've heard before. My best retort was: "Okay, then."

Petey, the beagle, watched this exchange with frank interest as she lay on the floor next to James William. Dogs and cats are aware of the spectral dimension, but Petey is the only four-legged fan of sunshine who sees us clearly. She also hears every word I say, which will come in handy once she understands that words are just a more complex way of barking.

I lowered myself through the floor to look into the dog's warm chocolate eyes. "Are shams a part of your life?" I asked the beagle. "Do you feel the need to act like an Irish Setter? Maybe a turn as a Chihuahua will put some gusto into your life."

The dog rolled onto her side and offered me the great favor of rubbing her belly, which I'm only too happy to provide, although, bearing in mind the differences between a beagle and a ghost, I must keep my spectral fingers from penetrating her skin. There's nothing relaxing about someone's thumb poking your appendix from the inside. Judging from Petey's reaction, my astral air massages are better than anything a Breather can offer.

At some point, James William clambered from the sofa, and Petey pulled herself to her feet and trotted behind him. I can't begrudge a friend who doesn't want to miss any tasty crumbs that might fall in her direction.

I kept my head and shoulders on the carpet and the rest of me dangling through the house's foundation and never took my eyes off the plastic figure hanging from the tree. Was that a knowing smirk on the soldier's face? The longer I looked, the better I came to understand the real Dawkins: his iron rectitude, the sense of determination, his assurance that comes from never meeting an obstacle he couldn't sidestep, ignore or intimidate, the anger barely contained under the placid veneer.

The hereafter is a no-rules zone, but one rule I insist upon having is that no one messes with my family.

So I didn't waste time when Hank showed up with the news that the line of spooks outside the Poe museum was longer than last night. I told him to start the auditions: I'd join him after taking care of something more important.

"More important than your legacy?" he asked.

I nodded and tried a question of my own. "How would you handle a spook-soldier who was making trouble for you? I've been thinking about calling on Heck's Angels for some spectral muscle. Or maybe Rosetta, for the damage that only a grammarian can do to your self-confidence."

"You've been in a 12-step program too long." Hank's pigtail nodded strongly in agreement. "You got a problem with someone in uniform? Take it up with his commanding officer."

CHAPTER Fifteen

The old routines had returned to the park at the end of the block. Spectral soldiers stretched on the ground despite the snow, their faces lined with fatigue, rifles pressed to their chests like slumbering babies. A few campfires flickered in the darkness. (How do they do that with ectoplasm?) Somewhere in the night, a harmonica played *Oh, Shenandoah*. (Ditto for a spook on a wind instrument.)

Making a quick survey, I didn't see the Colonel, so I asked the nearest spook who was in charge.

Without a word, he pointed his pipestem at a spook standing alone at the base of the memorial obelisk. The spook with all the stripes. As I approached, the sergeant spat a wad of ectoplasm that, no sooner had it splashed on the ground, slithered across the snow toward a boot and was reabsorbed into his astral figure.

"I'm looking for a certain spook who the Colonel says isn't in your unit," I told him. "But maybe he's assigned to some other outfit. If I lodge a complaint with you, perhaps you can pass my complaint to the right spooks."

"You're right on all accounts, mister." Sarge spat out another wad of black thingamaglob that hit the ground, splattered, then raced back into his boots. "The Colonel knows everyone in this regiment. If we don't have the spook you're looking for, I can see that your complaint gets passed up the chain of command. Headquarters can sort this out."

"That's very" — I looked at the grimy bayonet shoved under his belt — "civilized of you."

"What's the nature of your complaint?"

"He's been bothering a neighbor. The flesh and blood kind."

"Can't have any of that going on." Sarge nodded solemnly. "What's this trooper's name again?"

"Dawkins, Private Dawkins. I don't know his first name."

"That won't be necessary. I don't know it either. We call him Squawkin' Dawkin."

That news would've taken my breath away if I had any. Either Sarge knew more about other rebel units than the Colonel did. Or the Colonel had lied to me. Neither explanation made sense. The Colonel was the last one in the afterworld to be misinformed or misleading. There had to be a third possibility.

I stammered for a reply.

"Headquarters will be interested in your complaint," Sarge said. "Dawkins ain't on anyone's good side right now."

In a daze, I noticed Esmee waving over the sergeant's shoulder from the edge of the park. I thanked Sarge and headed toward her. For a quiet evening, there was no shortage of surprises. My favorite officer had feet of clay, as it were, and Esmee was able to function after her encounter last night with the embalming fluid.

Esmee linked arms with mine, waved toodle-oo to the troops and pulled me away, chattering all the while about how we're late for the party and our friends will be cross because they can't start the games without us.

The cloud of embalming fluid rising from Esmee could stun an astral ox, but I let her take me a half block from the hoots and catcalls of the troops before I shook myself loose.

"Will you stop talking nonsense," I said. "And while you're at it, quit dragging me around like a sack of rags. You're in no condition to take me anywhere."

"My condition is conditioned well enough to get you out of the condition you were just in."

"That spook was helping me. He was helping all of us. You shouldn't be rude to him."

"Rude, crude, shmude." She wavered in and out of focus. "I don't trust any Yankees."

"Yankees?" I gave her my best can-you-believe-this-drivel glare. "Whatever makes you think they're Yankees?"

Esmee steadied her gaze with both hands gripping her chin and said, "They got blue uniforms."

"If that's blue, then I'm a clueless, no-account, rock-solid, air-headed" – The wind puffed, the snow parted, and I saw soldiers loafing in the park in uniforms the color of a cloudless April morning – "Yankee."

For an instant, I swirled with the snowflakes. I had finally reached the time to retire to a quiet spot in the asteroid belt to work on my transcendence. I'd happily hang out there waiting for the universe as we know it to end.

Esmee swung her hip to get me behind a parked van. Waves of embalming smells swept over me. Spooks don't inhale but that doesn't keep odors from drifting into our nostrils.

I pushed her away to give my mind the chance to reboot. Yankees had snuck into the city and were behaving like they owned the place. And Dawkins was one of them. What happened to our brave defenders, the boys in gray, who've spent more than a century and a half protecting the city from northerners and their bad table manners?

"We've got to get the word out," I said. "We've got to warn everyone."

"I'm with you, chief."

Esmee shook her fists defiantly, although, owing to an excess of embalming fluid and a shortage of good sense, she jabbed her chin hard enough to send her eyeballs spinning in different directions. Flopping down on midair to recover, she left me to devise a plan by myself.

Where do you go when you're concerned about the safety of the streets, and you're somewhere that never had a police force, and the army you'd been counting on seems to be on a coffee break?

"Ahha, I know just the place," I said.

"What?" she queried.

I grabbed her hand and we left (*poof*) for greater problems.

THE HEADQUARTERS OF the Ace Acme Afterlife detective agency was a few blocks from the business district in a row of townhouses taken over by doctors, investment counselors and other professionals. Big G shared a desk with a lawyer, who paid the bills, oversaw the cleaning staff and occupied the offices during the daytime.

The Triple A also shared a secretary with the lawyer. Like Margie, Mrs. Pellywanger was a twofer who could baffle clients on more than one plane of existence. She was at her desk in the waiting room when Esmee and I slipped through the door. The place was otherwise empty, a rarity at this hour for a business that services the posthumous set.

Mrs. Pelly looked up from her computer, tapped a stack of notecards with her pencil and said, "Thank you for haunting. Your manifestation is important to us. Please take a number. You will be called in the order of your specterization."

She talked tough when the subject was a waiting list, but how would she react when she learned Yankees were prowling the streets of Richmond? I tested some language on my astral tongue, putting together the right combination of words and facial tics that'd get Mrs. Pelly to hop on her desk as though a tsunami of rats was gushing across her carpet.

Esmee chose that moment to assert herself. With her hip. Which nearly knocked me through the wall.

"We don't need a number." Esmee came out waggling her finger like a champ. "We are the only ones currently present at this point in time, right here."

Mrs. Pelly cut her a glance. "And I am the only one who can get you into the boss's office. Take a number."

I reached for the top card. My fingers sank through the stack and into her desktop as Esmee glared at the deck. No way was she soiling her ectoplasm by touching those cards.

Big G's voice rolled down the hall from the back offices. "Mrs. Pelly, have we got clients out there?"

"Let me check," she answered. Mrs. Pelly scanned the waiting room, pausing at each empty chair along the walls, even inspecting the uncluttered expanse of carpeting before settling on me.

"What is your number?"

I looked at my empty hand. "742."

"Go right in."

Big G had a wooden desk with the bronze name plate of the room's daytime occupant, Stuart Q. Stewart. Since my last visit, lawyer Stewart had acquired several stacks of worn, bulging folders. Having dealt with Stewart before, I was sure the folders contained law school essays, grocery receipts, investment advice, recipe clippings, the monthly bills and travel brochures.

Big G eyed Esmee coolly before asking me, "Do you think your friend ought to be here?"

Lawyer Stewart had been Esmee's first-life attorney. If Esmee hadn't realized that by now, chances are she never would. But Big G, despite his tough-guy demeanor, is the sort of spook who doesn't believe in taking chances with those kind of chances.

If Esmee picked up any echoes from her first life, they weren't important to her. She was on Big G so fast I was sure she wanted to share his cigar. "Are you going to tell me to take a number too?"

"Naw, wouldn't cross my mind, kid." He shifted the stogie to the other side of his mouth, putting extra distance between her and it. "There's poker games all over this city that need you."

Esmee drifted cautiously back through his desk and settled over a chair. The big palooka had earned some time by mentioning a magic word: poker. But she was reserving the right to let him know who's really boss.

"Something's been going on outside," I said. "While I was busy last night at the theater, the city got occupied."

Big G's droopy lids slumped further down his cheeks. "What do you mean?"

"I woke up this evening, Yankees were all over the place. Not a rebel in sight. I'd've noticed if my street turned into a battleground."

"That's not the sort of detail you'd miss." Big G's stogie nodded in agreement. "Thing is, I was out earlier and ran into a couple spooks I know from the Alabama Regiment. We was talking about plans for the holidays. You'd think they'd mention if they were planning to run away."

Esmee was back in his face. "Are you calling my friend a liar?"

"Not me, lady." Big G didn't miss a beat. "I'm saying not all the cards are on the table. *Capische?*"

"That I can understand."

As Esmee backed off, Big G must've felt his stogie was safe, for he laid out his plan. He'd touch base with his usual suspects; meanwhile, Esmee and I should go about our business, keeping an eye out for troop movements or, for that matter, troops standing around. We'd compare notes later at the theater.

"There's dozens of spooks waiting for their auditions at the Poe museum," I added, cringing at the memory of that line of hopeful smiles snaking across the parking lot. "I can fill them in and spread them across the city. They can let us know what they find out. Most of them'll appreciate the chance to do something."

Big G half-closed his eyes. Always a bad sign.

"And you're sure there's not a loose lip in the group? The kind that enjoys jabbering so much that a message gets delivered to the wrong ears?"

Esmee three-quarter-closed her eyes. "I've never trusted that bunch. They're just the kind who'll get a part, show up for rehearsals, then bug out on opening night. Can't count on them."

"You retired from the theater. Remember?" I told Esmee, while to Big G I added, "I get your point, boss."

Big G escorted us out of his office.

I used to be on the staff of the Triple A until my sponsor Cal decided it was interfering with my transcendence. I still missed the excitement, the lack of routine, the challenges, the confidence that let me feel I could pry the secrets from the shadows. The hereafter was less complicated when I solved its mysteries instead of wrestling with them.

"There's this soldier-spook named Dawkins," I told Big G. "He's with the spectral Union forces. Let me know if you pick up anything about him?"

"I'll add him to my list."

We went back in the waiting room. The spooks who'd been staying away in droves were continuing to show up absent. Big G slicked down the brim of his fedora. "I'd appreciate you wrapping up those auditions as soon as you can. They're – pardon the language, Miss – murdering my business. It's not worth getting up at night to come to the office. Meanwhile –"

" – Mum's the word," I added.

Mrs. Pelly was so busy scanning the waiting room for clients hiding behind chairs, curtains, curtain rods, door knobs and carpet fibers that I didn't bother to say good-bye.

Once we reached the front stoop, Esmee skittered around me like a spook who'd respecterized in a pepper jar. She grabbed my arm.

"Mum? You said *Mum* back there. We're going to see my Mum?"

$\mathscr{Sixteen}$
CHAPTER

A s Esmerelda and I skirted downtown and slipped across Shockoe Bottom, my mind wandered to a conversation I had long ago with Jedidiah, the first old-timer I met in Happily-Ever-After. He's one of those spooks who actually found his own grave and, consequently, never leaves the cemetery. *If you think some crisis is all about you,* Jedidiah told me once, stroking his long astral beard, *that's precisely when it has nothing to do with you.*

Shouldn't that mean if I'm sure some problem has nothing to do with me, that's when it really is about me? Like, to pull an example out of the nearest random hat, a sudden change in troop deployments. I can't think of anything that could possibly mean less to me. Which, by Jedidiah's way of reckoning, means it's crucial.

Peering into the darkest shadows below for signs of militarized spooks, I didn't spot a single uniform until we glided over the Poe museum and saw the specters lined up for their auditions. A few were dressed in red jackets and towering bearskin hats like the guards at Buckingham Palace; others were outfitted with gear appropriate for a Bronze Age difference of opinions.

Fast Eddie was working the crowd to entice the gamblers into placing ectoplasmic bets on their chances for getting a part in the play.

"I fancy a piece of that action," Esmee said, gliding down to Fast Eddie.

"And who's your favorite?" Fast Eddie asked. "Is it one of the Harry Potters? Perhaps a Cinderella? I see three strong candidates. Or maybe that large rabbit checking his pocket watch?"

Esmee gave him an elbow jab that, in a Sunshiner, would realign his spinal column. "I'm a player, not a sucker. Looks like you've got a new partner."

Before Fast Eddie could protest, Esmee followed up by giving him the hairy eye. Fast Eddie glanced at me for support. I gave him a supportive shrug.

A Christmas Wraith

"Take the back of the line," Fast Eddie said, in a rare burst of prudence. "I'll take the front. Quarter drop of ectoplasm per bet."

She flashed the sweetest smile, said, "And to think that one dies every minute," and hurried past the costumed actors waiting for their auditions.

Rather than run a gauntlet by cutting into line, I circled back to the street, darted into the museum's bookstore and came out in the courtyard as Hank was telling a performer decked out like Kermit the Frog that the director doesn't discriminate against anyone for being green.

"Yeah, but how many amphibians are in the cast?" mock-Kermit said. "Are you practicing species-ism?"

"Complaints of a legal nature go to Big G." Hank replied so smoothly that I knew he'd heard this threat before.

"Oh, okay," faux-Kermit said. "Just wondering."

"Next."

Rosetta was staffing the courtyard gate where the line of aspiring actors began. As she slipped outside to bring in the next candidate, I sidled over to Hank.

"How many contenders have we got so far?" I asked.

"Somewhere between zero and zilch."

"You're not being too tough on them, are you?"

"If you think this is easy, why don't you handle the next act," he said.

I agreed, but in fairness to me, Hank was looking over my shoulder and knew who – or what – was coming.

Mike the Cockatiel fluttered into the courtyard. Mike was the spirit of a dead bird who had found a place in the afterlife. Now he spends his time looking for formerly feathered fliers with whom he could put together a 12-step program. When I saw who was following him inside, I wondered why it had taken this long.

The Raven was a good nine or ten feet of glossy feathers and attitude. Its butter-colored beak managed a cynical sneer. Feet larger than Mike supported its lumbering frame.

"Let me see if I've got this straight," I mumbled to myself. "The Raven is the spectral manifestation of a fictional entity. Isn't that something like a double negative? Doesn't that mean the Raven operates on the physical dimension?"

"Whatever," the black bird said.

The Raven bent over the dried flower stems jutting from an oversized clay pot, and as its beak poked through the stems and desiccated leaf fragments, I heard a sound like ice cracking on a frozen lake.

Which would mean it was a physical entity. Which made as little sense as anything else that'd happened to me lately.

"Okay, show me your stuff." My eyes flicked from the Raven to Mike the Cockatiel and back again, not sure who was the actor and who the agent.

"Whatever," the Raven croaked.

Mike, who was perched on the air level with my chest, rolled his head to one side and stared at the Raven with a single glossy eye.

"WHATEVER," the Raven snapped again.

Mike jerked away, his head pivoted slowly up again until he was staring at me.

"Whatever," the Raven said, more softly.

Mike flipped onto his back.

"I get it," Hank said. "It's a comedy act."

I edged away. Comics get testy when audiences need explanations for their jokes. But this duo relaxed after Hank's observation. Guess it helped their confidence to know someone understood what they were trying to do, even if we didn't double over with belly laughs.

Their routine got smoother, snappier. The Raven would say "Whatever," Mike would react, and at the end of each bit, Mike would fall on his chest or float on his head or spread his wings with the universal gesture requesting help from the Uber-Spirit.

When Hank glanced at his arm where a Breather would carry a wristwatch, the Raven and Mike the Cockatiel speeded up their last gag like true professionals and concluded with a coordinated bow.

I had to clap. "Wonderful, wonderful. You kids have a great future ahead of you. Thanks for taking the time to show us your stuff. We'll get back to you after we firm up our plans for the cast. But I gotta tell you: You guys were terrific, just terrific."

The birds fluttered way, jabbering like magpies. Rosetta ducked into the parking lot to retrieve the next candidate for an audition, and Hank turned to me.

"Can't you picture the big guy showing up with the Ghost of Christmas Future? Or maybe as one of Santa's helpers."

"We can't go mixing our fairy tales. It's tough enough working just with spooks and Sunshiners." I watched the Raven in the distance balloon in size to step over a pickup by the curb. "Let's put them on the *maybe* list."

Chug-a-chug-chug. Wooo-WOOO.

Speaking of mixing fairy tales, up the path from the courtyard gate came Rosetta with an engine of the toot-toot variety, a railroad engine, whose ectoplasmic chassis was formed from the fragments of dozens of holiday stories. One of its gyrating wheels was, on closer inspection, a wooden crutch lurching up the walkway, while the next axle had an angel's wing that flapped with a steady rhythm, and in place of a third wheel was the gleaming blade of a sled.

Beribboned boxes towered over the coal car, along with the odd elf and a few scruffy Victorian youngsters who couldn't take their eyes off the smokestack and the plume where a star raced above the dark and trackless sky. The front of a proper railroad engine would have a headlight, but this phantasmagoric contraption had a bulbous reddish glow that was not unlike a nose. In fact, a nose is precisely what it was.

If the train hadn't smiled at me, I might not have been concerned. But it did and I recognized the smile.

Still, we had promised to give all comers a fair chance, so I told the engine to show us what it could do, and as Hank and I stood in the courtyard of the Poe museum, the engine circled us with many a *chug-chug-chug*. The elves waved and the star above the smokestack twinkled and the crutch on the front axle thumped and the cabin's silver bells jingled and whenever the boiler door swung open I heard a tune so soft and wonderful it could only have come from an angelic choir.

Hank had to call "Time" three or four times, and even then *The Little Engine That Might* didn't stop until I stepped directly in its tracks.

"Fantastic job," I said, reaching for the smokestack. "We'll call you and let you know."

My astral fingers pincered the stack, the little train said, "Ouch," and Esmerelda's ectoplasmic ear respecterized in my hand, with the rest of Esmee attached and squirming.

"I thought we had an agreement," I said. "If you quit trying to get into the play, I'd find you a good card game."

"Those college boys were no fun," she whined. "All they do is sit around and read law books. It's hard to concentrate on the game with that racket going on."

Hank and I exchanged a look. Law books? At the frat house?

"I'll make you a deal," I said. "Since the frat house is too tame, I'll introduce you to some spooks whose idea of fun is a little more . . . ah . . . What's the word I'm looking for?"

Hank saw where I was going. "Cataclysmic."

"That's it. Cataclysmic. But it'll cost you. In addition to keeping your nose out of my play, you're going to be at our Specters Anonymous meeting tonight. Deal?"

"Honey, I'm always ready to deal, make a deal or be deal-icious."

Hank and I did a group groan.

$\mathscr{S}$eventeen
CHAPTER

$\mathscr{T}$he location of the Squid's Beak Inn is controversial even among its regulars. The consensus puts it along the water, although there's a divergence of views about the body of water in question, with an obnoxious minority asking why anyone would want to question a river and an inflexible faction insisting the waterway in dispute is smaller than a river, again with differing blocs advocating a water hazard at a golf course (with further subdivisions over the specific course implicated), various local streams, the outdoor pool at several community centers, decorative fountains in three plazas and a ruptured sewage pipe in Jackson Ward.

Me? I just go to the James River, look upstream and down, studying both banks until I find the densest spot of fog hugging the shore, then head in that direction. Before long I'm enveloped in swirling patches of gray, and regardless of the route I take from there, I know that soon a warped, clapboard-sided building will rise from the mist like a long-lost mausoleum.

Inside, the air was only marginally clearer. A bar ran along a wall, the bartender stood with his back to the customers for as long as possible, and the few clients – whether physical or astral – hunched over their drinks and minded their own business. It's the sort of place where the shadows had shadows and the silence kept to itself.

"Neat-o," Esmerelda said. "Why've you been keeping this joint a secret?"

The customers crouched further over their drinks, while the bartender adjusted his work to make sure the center of his spine stayed pointing at us.

Esmee sidled to the nearest guy on a barstool. "Hey, buddy, where's the action?" She slapped his shoulder; her hand slid through his body and emerged from his sternum. "A Sunshiner," she grunted. "That's disappointing."

The customer didn't react, but I felt an icy wave ripple through me when her fingers wriggled from his chest like worms on a hook. How could a Breather be indifferent to an arm's worth of spectral essence rubbing against every organ north of his abdominal cavity? It wasn't normal. It wasn't even paranormal.

"We're going this way," I told Esmee.

Reluctantly, she followed me around tables and chairs that were scattered across the floor by the last fight. The embalming fluid Esmee found at the frat house must have been wearing off because I didn't have to explain that this was the sort of place she wanted to avoid drifting through physical objects. The hollowed-out leg of a table filled with cremated remains was, by any calculation, a grave, and a spook who ventured into one wasn't going to venture out.

A door loomed over the back wall. I held up my hand and listened. Nothing disturbed the silence behind the door. Just my luck: the gang had already left for their nightly jaunt. Still, we'd come this far, so Esmee might has well see what the afterlife looks like for some spooks.

I nodded toward that door, and the next instant we respecterized in a room six or seven times larger than the rest of the building. A line of spooks in black leather jackets glared at us like panthers waiting for the lunch truck to arrive. Each spook straddled a spectral motorcycle that wasn't there, at least not in most meanings of *there*.

A burly fellow in the middle of the line tweaked a handlebar, his bike went *AAAGGRRRRR* and the big guy opened his mouth with each roar, perfectly timed, so that by the third growl I wasn't sure whether the rider or the bike was making the noise. That was Red Max, biker-in-chief for Heck's Angels, the afterlife's most notoriously uncivil collection of ectoplasm, whose members believe that being dead was just another long, open highway.

Red Max eased his spectral Harley closer and gunned the engine. "If you've come to take us to a meeting, we're not going without a fight."

"Actually, that's not why I'm here," I offered.

"Wait a minute," Esmee chimed. "I'd like to see how this gentlespook handles a temper tantrum."

Red Max grinned. His smile was more unnerving than his glower. "Me and the boys are planning a short cruise along the Piedmont at Mach 7. Want to come?"

The invitation was for Esmee. The evil grin was for me.

Esmee beamed. "Where have you been all my afterlife? You're my kind of spooks."

A chorus of bellowing engines greeted her. This was turning out exactly the way I'd planned, which was flat-out unnerving. Cal has warned me more than once, *You should always make a plan. That way you'll have something to complain about once things fall apart.*

"Remember to bring Esmee back," I told Red Max.

Instantly, I regretted being in the vicinity of any combination of words that remotely resembled instructions for the biker chief. Sparks flew from the ends of the big guy's mustache and beard; his eyeballs went totally dark, and I could've believed they were having their own eclipse. He leaned over his handlebars for a closer look at me.

"You're the spook who's putting together that play," he said.

I braced myself. Everyone wants to be a critic, but some critics are more likely than others to see if they could rearrange the body parts of a brother spook.

As it turned out, I was bracing for the wrong attack.

A shadow rolled over Red Max. He rose on his bike's footpegs. Something happened to his cheeks and forehead that might have been an ethereal glow or, perhaps, a poorly placed kind of diaper rash.

He said: *"Juliet, O Juliet! Wherefore art thou, Juliet?"*

At that moment, Red Max was a hopeful child. A very large child with a red beard and scowling features, but a child nonetheless, who deserved to hear the truth in a gentle way.

"That was nicely done. Very professional," I said. "But, you know, actually the line is: *Romeo, O Romeo! Wherefore art thou, Romeo?*"

"Says who?"

Red Max knelt on the handlebars now, his fiery facial hair lit up the back room. Thunder rumbled from his mouth with sufficient fury to shake the ceiling and floor and everything in between.

"Absolutely," I added. "Who says a dead Englishman always gets the last word? That was the best line I've heard since"— Red Max's look loaded me with enough caution to last for several afterlives —"since the last time you had a best line."

"And you know about best lines?" the biker challenged.

"I know them all: Best lines, fine lines, red lines, tight ropes, nooses." I didn't like the direction my mouth was taking me. "Let me check with my colleagues. I'm not sure which roles are still open."

"You do that."

Red Max twitched a corner of his mouth, Esmee climbed behind him on the Harley, his motorcycle snarled and shuddered, and the leader of Heck's Angels led his pack spiraling into the night air. I stood at attention with a hand on my chest as the cavalcade swept past. Even an astral parade needs spectators on the sidelines or it's just another bunch of folks leaving for somewhere else.

After the last biker roared through the ceiling, all traces of Heck's Angels faded into the shadows. Toolboxes, spare tires and puddles of oil on the wood floor, everything dissolved into the night, and the room shrank to the dimensions of a storage closet in the back of the Squid's Beak Inn.

CAREFULLY, I PICKED my way through furniture strewn across the main room of the inn. At least I'd kept Esmee from stumbling across anything from her first life for another night. Each overturned chair and shattered table leg was evidence of a vigorous discussion among Breathers, the likes of which were denied to those of us who'd already attended our own wakes.

For the first time since coming to the hereafter, I understood why a spook might get this far from his expiration date and still want to chuck it all for a few moments to smash plates and flip small rocks onto the roofs of houses.

Easing around a mangled table, I spotted a bottle of catsup on the bar. My spectral fingers twitched as I imagined crossing the transdimensional barrier and seizing that bottle with a grip that an army of Breathers couldn't shake, then hurling it through the front window.

I could visualize glass fragments spraying into the night and tentacles of catsup reaching out to squeeze the shadows. A cacophony of glistening splinters splashed on the sidewalk, I imagined, and a layer of shimmery shards dropped on the window sill as the night filled with an otherworldly tinkling, so soft, so fragile, yet embedded with the memory of a sharp, darting pain.

A dark figure moving behind the bar pulled me from my reverie. "What'll you have?" the bartender asked.

"Postmortal peace. Spooks who take care of themselves but never try to control others. Lines of communication that stay open even on this side of the grave. Egos that are checked at the cemetery gates. And a nickel cigar."

"I am confident of progress on the first four items," the bartender said. "As for the cigar, that may present difficulties."

"What would you suggest?"

"Have you considered being cut in half by a razor-sharp pendulum?"

I looked into weary, haunted eyes. "How does that help anything?"

"I understand it effectively activates one's problem-solving abilities." The bartender, known most evenings as Edgar Allan Poe, swiped an astral cleaning cloth across the bar.

The mirror behind the poet was coated with the grime of decades and framed by liquor bottles with labels curled with age. A lone pink paper umbrella, no larger than a daisy, was wedged between keys of the antique cash register.

Poe's brow added a wrinkle or two. "Does my vocabulary exceed the grasp of your understanding? Again? Which words do you wish me to simplify?"

"It's not your vocabulary I'm worried about. It's your motivation."

"Whatsoever could possibly be troublesome about that?"

"You're being nice just to get your grabby little hands on my play."

"Grabby? GRABBY? From which dialect of the King's English comes that perky little gem to confuse the unlettered masses?" Poe gave the ruffles of his shirt a consoling tug. "As for the substance of your insinuation, I have not the slightest interest in tarnishing my reputation by any involvement with your alleged theatrical production."

"My *alleged* play? Who's taking liberties with language now?" I hoisted myself from the floor for effect. "It's got a script. It's got a cast. It's got costumes. What more does a play need to become non-alleged?"

Poe tapped his dainty lips with the head of his silver cane. "Hmm. Does it have a theater?"

"Of course it does." In my mind's eye, I saw again the spotlight hurtling from the darkness to pulverize the mock-door on the stage. "Doesn't it?"

"To quote from my favorite masterpiece of American literature," he said, "*Nevermore.*"

$\mathscr{E}$ighteen

CHAPTER

$\mathscr{L}$ ess than a second after leaving Edgar Allan Poe and the haunted grounds of the Squid's Beak Inn *(poof)*, I pulled myself together *(repoof)* inside the Byrd Theater.

Silence and darkness overwhelmed the interior, from the folding seats in the audience to the empty orchestra pit and the equally barren and dark stage on which my favorite fraternity was supposed to be rehearsing its Christmas play.

An eighth sense drew me to glance at the balcony. A distinctive face composed of sharp angles and flat surfaces that could've been made with a trowel gazed down at me.

I was on him quicker than a two-year-old on a birthday cake.

"You there! Dawkins! Stay right where you are."

The soldier didn't move, but he managed to stay put in a way that let me know his immobility had nothing to do with my insistence that he shouldn't go anywhere.

Zooming near the ceiling with the balcony railing between us, I took stock of my adversary. My enemy. Usually, I wouldn't talk like that about another spook around Cal or Rosetta or a regular from my 12-step program, but for too long, whenever something went wrong (or simply failed to go right) Dawkins had been lurking in the background.

His uniform reminded me of the Somber Sisters with their ashen robes, seemingly an accumulation of ashes, devoid of significant features. With Dawkins, I couldn't make out much more than the general location of the buttons on his coat and the insignia on his collar and shoulders, making him a spook who could get chewed out by the officers of opposing armies for having a sloppy uniform.

Speaking of chewing, I had a bone to pick with this spook.

"You were at my house. Talking to the little boy who lives there. Don't deny it."

"Okay," he said, smooth as silk.

"If you ever go there again, you'll wish you hadn't. You'll look for a spotlight factory for your next vacation. For the peace and quiet."

"Don't worry, I'll mind my own business."

"Speaking of spotlights, I saw what you did at the theater. Dropping that spotlight on the stage."

"It won't happen again."

"It better not," I snapped.

Dawkins lifted a hand in a half-hearted farewell and drifted through the ceiling, neither glancing back nor giving the slightest hint that he was anything except a peaceable spirit tending his own affairs, and I found myself thinking that I've never had less satisfaction from winning an argument. The spook didn't even have the decency to stay put for a volcanic eruption while I chided him for hiding his Union affiliation behind that soiled uniform.

I was surprised to realize I wanted a titanic clash of wills. Getting a dope to admit that he was wrong and he'd change his ways wasn't enough: I wanted drama, screaming, whimpering and pleas for mercy, threats and counter-threats, expressions that bruised and voices that cut like a chain saw going through a plywood box.

"Looks like you already got the word," said Hank, respecterizing on the front row of the balcony.

I haven't gotten any words lately, I wanted to say. But I still had a bunch of words, a deluge, an avalanche, enough words with nowhere to go to make an ectoplasmic entity pop. *Restraint of fist and spit* is one of the enduring maxims of my 12-step program, and this seemed like a good time to apply that principle.

"Exactly what word are we talking about?" I asked.

"Liability," Hank said.

"Sounds like someone needs a competent lawyer."

The pigtail at the back of Hank's neck was relaxed, and I could tell he felt the situation was under control, even if it wasn't heading in the direction I wanted.

"Actually," he said, "in this case, I think a reckless lawyer would be better."

"Ain't that usually what happens?"

We headed back toward the business district at a Breather's pace, and Hank gave me the details. He'd been overseeing the auditions at the Poe museum when some spooks said the frat brothers were disassembling the sets at the theater and carting away their gear. He left Rosetta in charge of the tryouts and hustled to the theater to get the straight scoop.

I'd heard enough. "Thanks to Dawkins and the falling spotlight, the frat boys are afraid of being sued, and they don't have the money to buy liability insurance."

"Bingo," Hank said.

Then why didn't I feel like I'd bingoed? Edgar Allan Poe was no longer interested in weaseling his way into my theatrical production. The mysterious Private Dawkins was so eager not to give offense that I was about to invite him to Rosetta's next course on assertiveness for the afterlife. And a house filled with college-aged men, whose idea of a good time involved spreading chaos and confusion throughout the city, was pondering the implications of being responsible. What more could I expect them to do? Sit up straight and not talk with their mouths full of beer?

"What's wrong with this picture?" I mused.

"Just a little touch-up, here and there." Hank was all confidence. "We make sure anyone who tries to sue them in the first-life regrets it. In our world, Big G will volunteer to show troublemakers some muscle."

I shot him a look. "By *muscle*, you mean hiding in the shadows and yelling, *Boo*."

"You gotta start someplace."

But Hank was on the right track. We were nearly at the clock tower by the railroad station. A thin blanket of snow lay across the city and reflected enough light to make a self-respecting spook feel jittery. I reversed course and headed back downtown, with Hank hot on my astral heels.

If you can't count on a fraternity for a mayhem, what are you going to do? I had some ideas.

HOLIDAY SPECIAL — TWO Consultations for the Price of One was the hand-lettered sign on the iron fence surrounding the townhouse that Big G shared with lawyer Stuart Q. Stewart. The clients who'd been avoiding the Triple A detective agency still continued to flock elsewhere.

Hank and I found Big G and his twofer secretary Mrs. Pellywanger hunched over Mrs. Pelly's desk in the waiting room. A couple kindergarten classes could've been stocked with the crayons and thick papers strewn across the table.

"Take a number," she said.

"391."

"You're next."

"Actually," Big G said, rising from the desk like a whale breaching after a long dive. "I'll see you now."

Hank and I followed him down the hallway to his office while Big G explained that he'd convinced Mrs. Pelly to do some advertising, hence the sign outside that appeals to both spectral and first-life customers. Holiday crowds were always interested in bargains, and maybe they'd jump for a two-for-one offer before fully realizing that neither Big G's services nor lawyer Stuart Q. Stewart's were the sort of things that go under a Christmas tree with a nifty red bow.

That's the attention to detail that made Big G the afterlife's top shamus. No sooner had he settled behind the desk in the big office than he adjusted his cigar stub and lowered his eyelids.

"What do you want me to do for your play?" he said. "And why should I help you?"

My mouth worked like a guppy's. Bad moment to remember that Big G blamed the Christmas play for a drop in his business.

"I was in the area and wanted to say, *Happy Holidays*," I said. "So, Happy Holidays. Don't let me take up any more of your time."

"It's about the liability insurance, isn't it?" Neither Big G nor his stogie nor his lowered eyelids moved.

I glanced at Hank. He gave me a confident grin. I tried to clear my throat even though I haven't had an actual throat for a long time, but that didn't keep me from wondering what Henry Kissinger would say in this situation.

"I can't ask you to help a play that's hurting your business."

"Yes, you can." Big G's stogie moved by itself to the other side of his mouth where the view was better. "You're forgetting the code."

"Ah, the PI code."

The fine print in the Paranormal Investigator's Code came flooding back from my nights working for the Triple A. The case comes first, the case always comes first, although exceptions are made for a wounded partner, a dame in distress or a free drink of rot-gut. (*Note to readers: Maybe it's time to simplify the code. Let's start with the premise that what comes first is a female partner with a medical condition, a bottle in her hand and an assignment under her belt. Now, isn't that clearer?*)

"I was thinking," I told Big G, "that if the frat boys can't afford insurance to pay for a lawyer, how about cutting out the middleman and sending them directly to the lawyer?"

The stogie, sensing where I was going, pointed to Stuart Q. Stewart's name plate on the desk.

"And how, exactly, is this lawyer going to find out about the deal?" Big G asked, never one to bother with the big picture when a couple vexatious details are flapping in the wind, in this instance, the inability of spooks to communicate with most folks in the physical world. "And, while we're looking at imponderables, who lets the college kids know that we've got their back?"

I rolled my eyes until they focused in the general direction of the empty waiting room.

Big G's jowls drooped a little further, the stogie hurried to the center of his mouth. "Mrs. Pelly is hitting her career peak as we speak, working with crayons and drawing paper. Having a pulse isn't enough to get the job done."

"But it doesn't hurt to try," Hank offered.

"With Mrs. Pelly, it could hurt plenty," he said. "If it's a twofer we need, how about Ralph having a chat with his buddy Margie?"

The big guy arranged his ham-sized spectral hands on the desk and closed his eyes. The cigar stub wandered from one corner of his mouth to the other in a fair replication of nervous pacing.

Hank was watching me so carefully that even a spook who wasn't trained at the Triple A could suspect I was under surveillance. Hank knew the score between Margie and me, and that meant he knew the dangers of pushing us together.

"Good," I said and the word rang like a gavel hitting the judge's bench. "Margie and the lawyer know each other. They got along when Stewart handled Esmee's will. I'll talk to her."

Before anyone decided to tinker with a workable solution, I ushered Hank and myself out of the office while Big G helped his cigar stub find a comfortable resting place on his lower lip.

Then we reached Mrs. Pelly's domain.

The secretary held up her hand as I glided into the waiting room. "Please take a number and wait to be called."

Hank came within inches of her nose. "We're on our way out, sister. You're not trying to tell us we need a number to leave, are you?"

"If I'm not mistaken, that's exactly what I told you." Mrs. Pelly looked over the rim of her granny-style reading glasses (When did she start wearing glasses?) and added: "And don't call me *sister*."

I guess things were going too smoothly.

ℐineteen
CHAPTER

f a spook hadn't wandered into the detective agency looking for help finding a buddy, Hank and I might still be cooling our astral heels at Mrs. Pelly's desk.

All our problems were on the cusp of a solution. Before the sun opens for business in a few hours, I could look at the last seconds of *The Honeymooner's* DVD, learn the fateful lesson that's been delaying my transcendence and *poof* out of here before the automatic timers on Richmond's coffeepots start beeping. But first I had to get Margie to talk to lawyer Stewart about resolving the fraternity's legal problems with renting the theater, thus allowing the play to go on and leaving me a legacy that would be remembered in future holidays.

"Do you think anyone's still hanging around the Poe museum for auditions?" I asked Hank after we reached the sidewalk outside the Triple A.

"With Rosetta in charge?" he said. "She's probably still critiquing their costumes."

"You should go back and handle the auditions. I'll talk to Margie."

Hank didn't move. The pigtail at the back of his head didn't move either. He looked at me through half-closed eyelids and said, "I got a better idea. How about you talk to Margie, and I'll handle the auditions."

I slapped my forehead. "Why didn't I think of that? That's the perfect solution. Thanks, Hank."

"Nothing to it."

Fast Eddie once told me that pride keeps growing like hair and fingernails after a guy's been fitted for his own casket. For once, Fast Eddie might have known what he was talking about.

Hank left for the museum where hopefuls must be lined up for their moment of onstage glory, and I went in the opposite direction toward Carytown and the flickering *Psychic Advisor* sign in Margie's window that lent a measure of holiday cheer to the snow-covered streets and tiny lawns.

Did you ever walk into a graveyard and discover that not a spook there will talk to you? Okay, bad example. But you'll understand my reaction when, outside Margie's waiting room, I heard the shouting, joking, yakking and generalized racket of a crowd of spooks, then once I was inside all conversations ended in mid-yak, jaws froze open and I could look down several gullets to the tops of the owner's toes. Not a single pair of eyeballs, nay, not a solitary wayward eyeball, strayed in my direction.

"Evening," I said, cheerily. "Wonderful night out there. Don't you just love these crisp winter evenings?"

A few mouths pursed in sour smiles, a couple of backs became less rigid, one head even nodded, and the conversations resumed, although without the gusto they had before and without anyone stooping to acknowledge my presence.

I eased toward the window sill where the world's ugliest vase was entwined by a string of twinkling Christmas lights.

"So this is what it's like to forget my deodorant," I mumbled to myself.

"Couldn't say."

From the purple vase came the squeaky, ever-fawning voice of Sniveler, one of the spooks entombed in the ceramics who believed I was a divinity.

"I thought you weren't talking to me," I said.

"Can't say that either."

"But you *are* saying that you can't say that," I answered. "Isn't that saying something?"

"Darn. I knew I shouldn't bandy words with a godhead."

"Let that be a lesson to you."

When I turned around, the room's spooks were exactly as they'd been before my chat with Sniveler, but now many had costumes: elves, Elvises, Oliver Twists, Star Wars figures, characters from Disney movies and Marvel comics, even a few werewolves, vampires and insurance salesmen.

If I didn't move soon, I'd be up to my spectral ears in spooks clamoring for the chance to show why they deserved major roles in *A Christmas Carol*. Like a politician in desperate need of a rest room, I worked my way through the crowd without inviting conversation.

"Good to see you again. Wonderful outfit. Where've you been hiding? Say *Hello* to the missus."

Clearing the waiting room and finally reaching the hall beyond that led to the suite's other offices, I discovered a single spook sitting opposite Margie at her table in her room. That conversation, too, ended the moment I arrived. I smiled encouragingly at Margie and when I looked back at her client, the spook had converted some of his ectoplasm into a coonskin cap, pelt jacket and pants, and a spectral muzzleloader that reached the ceiling.

"Howdy, partner," the spook said. "Betcha' fancy an old-time holiday. With squirrels roasting on the spit and a little brown jug cooling in a snowdrift. When men were men, women were men, and kids would look at a reindeer with a shiny red nose and think: *Steaks for breakfast*."

I patted my hands together. "A traditional American Christmas. What a marvelous idea. This deserves serious consideration. By the way, you know my colleague Hank is taking care of all auditions at the Poe Museum. I'm sure he'd be – "

Quicker than you can say, *Lights, camera, action*, the chair was empty.

"Was it something I said?"

Margie cocked her head to a shoulder. "To coin a phrase, '*Natch*."

For a business owner who didn't have a single paying customer in her waiting room, Margie was relaxed, and now that I thought about it, in all our time together I haven't seen her hold onto an upbeat mood for more than fifteen seconds.

"You're happy," I said. "What's wrong?"

"Just enjoying the season. I'm really looking forward to seeing your play."

"Funny you should mention that."

So I filled her in on my problem. The fraternity putting on the holiday pageant couldn't afford liability insurance, and perhaps she could talk to lawyer Stewart about helping the frat boys if they ran into legal difficulties.

"I'll contact him in the morning. He seemed like a reasonable guy when he handled Sophie's will," she said. "Excuse me, I keep forgetting she's Esmee now."

"Perfectly understandable."

Margie was studying me, the corners of her eyes crinkled with amusement. What was going on? Had I put my legs on backward again? Or had something happened that was more personal? Dare I say, intimate?

"How's your friend, the newspaper reporter, doing?" I asked. "I haven't seen him for a while."

"Scoop was here for an early supper. Gotta work the late shift."

Margie's gaze was steady, sparkly. I called upon my keen investigative instincts to examine my friend for those clues that even the craftiest adversary can't hide from a PI. Was that cryptic half-smile an indication of relief that a relationship was over? Or that it was proceeding nicely? Perhaps her boyfriend had discovered that the way to Margie's heart was paved with Rocky Road ice cream?

Then again, the grin on da Vinci's masterpiece was known in certain circles as a Margie-the-Psychic smile. Maybe I should trust my investigative skills less and my paranoia more.

"If I didn't know you better," I said, "I'd think you just heard something interesting about me."

"But you do know me better. And I have learned something about you."

"What is it?"

"I'll give you a clue." Margie's Mona Lisa smile became a Bozie the Clown smirk. "I watched the end of your *Honeymooners* DVD."

Perhaps a lesser spook, hearing Margie's confession, would have pressed her to find out what was on the disc or zipped into her private apartment at the end of the hall where she keeps her DVDs and scooted around that disc until all the bits and bytes fell into place.

I, however, am not a lesser spook. I'm committed to leaving a legacy in the afterlife if it's the last thing I do, although I know it won't be the *final* last thing I do, an honor that falls to the lesson embedded in the concluding seconds of that sitcom.

With a smile containing as much confidence as I could muster, I drifted down the hall, turned left into the waiting room, and went out the door and onto the sidewalk. To keep going felt like a great idea. The polar vortex was brisk this time of year and, besides, there's nothing like riding a jet stream to put your problems into a fresh perspective.

Hundreds of spooks streaked across the northeast as the New Caledonia Precision Spectral Flying Team assembled for a practice session for their holiday show. I get a warm tingle wherever my heart's supposed to be as those spooks filled the sky with an awesome replica of reindeer pulling a sleigh. When they were directly over the city, they transformed into a gigantic star, then an angel, then exploded into a gazillion tiny packages, each coming down on a teeny golden parachute with a red bow and a handwritten name tag, drifting as gently as doves' feathers to the homes below. It's worth the price of admission to the hereafter to see the Spectral Flying Team put on a show.

Not wanting to interfere with their rehearsal, I went in the opposite direction to the top of the Omni Hotel where a familiar dark figure looked down from the roof.

The Colonel nodded as I arrived. "I believe you have come in time to observe the unfolding events."

I glanced over my shoulder at the flying team, which was still pulling in members from the countryside. "As often as I've seen this, I'm still excited to watch them perform."

"Those boys make us all proud, but I'm referring to the evening's other fireworks."

The Colonel leaned over the low concrete wall that enclosed the roof. On two sides of the 6th Street intersection below, spooks in gray uniforms had taken positions, their long rifles pointing at a bend where Cary Street sloped down to Shockoe Bottom. Despite the layer of snow on the ground, a fog bank was working its way up from the river.

"Oh my gosh, I haven't had the chance to tell you about the new patrols. And this infiltrater."

The Colonel didn't take his eyes off the troops below. "Would you be referring to northern units in our city? Patrolling like they owned the place? Perhaps even occupying the memorial where I usually plant my flag?"

"So, you know they've snuck into the city?"

"Snuck?" An eyelid twitched gently on the Colonel's forehead. "*Followed our bait* would be a more apt description."

I've never underestimated the Colonel, but at that moment, watching the fog build on the street like a wave captured on a slow-motion film, I realized I'd failed to appreciate the spook's true depths.

CHAPTER

Twenty

nce reassembled in the sky above the distant fair ground, the New Caledonia Precision Spectral Flying Team headed inland toward the Blue Ridge Mountains to continue practicing their holiday performance without giving away any surprises to onlookers, leaving the Colonel and me to watch without distraction the drama unfolding on the streets below.

For the longest time, nothing happened. Late night traffic on the interstate looping around the city to the east and south consisted mostly of utility trucks spreading salt and sand to keep the bridge surfaces from freezing. A few intrepid pedestrians strolled on the sidewalks to enjoy the winter-wonderland atmosphere, outnumbering the cars that threaded their way through downtown.

From the hotel rooftop, I almost missed the hazy bundle that floated out of the wall of fog at the end of the street. Smaller than a basketball, it drifted three or four feet above the cobblestones.

The Colonel read my perplexity without looking up. "GPS. Geographic Paranormality Spectrograph. Whoever's coming is unfamiliar with the city."

"Ah."

Behind the GPS, a rifle muzzle poked from the fog and rocked slowly from side to side like the chains on Gilda's Goth jacket. A second muzzle followed, then a third.

By the time a spook stepped from the mist, rifle in hand, I didn't need the Colonel to explain what was going on. Even from this distance, the dark blue uniforms stood out like ink blots on the snow. A Union patrol that had been moving with the fog bank was now slipping from their concealment. Anxiously, I studied each face, looking for Private Dawkins's angular features.

The Colonel laid a hand on my shoulder. Before I could thank him for the reassurance, he pushed down hard and kept pressing until my ectoplasmic legs slid through the roof and my knees rested on the asphalt topping.

Eight spectral Yankees emerged from the fog and glided forward. None of them was Dawkins. Their rifles swept the store fronts, parked cars, side streets, trees planted along the sidewalks, even some college kids snuggling in the shadows of a restaurant's door frame who were believers of the make-love-not-war philosophy.

The Confederates at the intersection — there were four of them, each sunk into the brick walls and cement sidewalk until little protruded except their heads, trigger fingers and rifles — adjusted their aim to track the progress of the enemy.

"Those Yankees might be dead," I opined, "but they're still not going to know what hit them."

"Son, you've always struck me as a coffin-half-filled kind of spook." The Colonel's gaze was steady, although a wary wrinkle furrowed the corners of his eyes. "My boys will give them something far worse than a shellacking."

I was no strategist, but the Colonel wasn't making sense. "What's tougher on the Yankees than a righteous whopping?"

"Keep your eyes on my boys," he said. "You never know when you'll be called to defend our way of death."

By inches and feet, the Union patrol approached the hidden rebels. By microns and millimeters, the Confederates dissolved into sidewalks and buildings. When the Yankees reached the intersection, the spectral boys in gray were gone.

"That's it? That's your idea of defending the city?"

The Colonel allowed himself a small smile. "You've just witnessed a textbook maneuver, straight from the classic *Art of Spectral Warfare*. As Digitalis says, *Confusion is the master of the battlefield. Never stand between the enemy and his own confusion.*"

"But they didn't fight!"

"True. Neither did we help the enemy by clarifying the situation he's facing on the ground. He'll have to deal with his own confusion by himself."

Peering from the rooftop of the multistory hotel, I saw the Yankee patrol milling around the intersection. They must have suspected that they were heading into an ambush, for they scuffed their astral boots into concrete, asphalt and cobblestones, trying to decide whether they'd been overly cautious.

Yankees stared down the vacant streets, rifle butts at their shoulders, poised to unleash a blizzard of spectral minie balls at the first suspicious shadow.

In the center of the street, a soldier looked up. His eyes widened, his jaw dropped, a finger jabbed the night air, pointing at the Colonel and me on the roof.

"Another observation from Digitalis comes to mind," the Colonel said. "*When you're outnumbered, leave immediately for an area where the odds are better.*"

The old soldier nodded at the hut-like structure on the roof that housed cables and winches for the elevators. When the enemy scooted up the sides of the building, the Colonel and I plummeted down the shaft.

Once in the basement, he dipped his hat before darting into the shadows. I had the option of plunging through the wall after him and making my way back home, ten or twenty feet underground. Which, for a city like Richmond whose roots go back three or four centuries, carried the risk of stumbling into an old casket and spending the rest of eternity in a decomposing box with the ghost of a colonial-era housewife interested in hearing about the latest innovations in stain removal.

I could think of safer ways to travel. Squeezing myself to the size of a snowflake, I floated up a staircase, across the lobby and out the hotel's main glass doors.

The storm had ended hours ago, but gusts from the south whisked flakes from the ground, from car fenders and the crosspieces of iron fences and whirled everything together in a cloud of confectionery wonder — as though a flour bag had burst inside a tornado — and I made a mental note to get out more when it's snowing, that's assuming the next stage of my transcendence includes weather. You don't need a heartbeat to enjoy snowflakes.

Twirling and skipping above the city, I eventually reached the memorial near the duplex that I shared with Gilda, where the grounds near the obelisk were deserted, and I fought the urge to circle the monument a few more times. I can get dizzy enough, thank you very much, without outside influences.

Respecterizing in what I thought was my favorite duplex, I found myself in another fog bank. I had traded a world of vivacious cottony glimmers for a dull gray mush, although, giving these grim surroundings some credit, the Christmas tree in the corner twinkled and sparkled for all it was worth.

The Christmas tree helped me get my bearings. I was in the right place. It was the Somber Sisters who were lost.

I had never seen more than three members of that silent, ashen sisterhood at one time, but now several dozen Somber Sisters were packed into the living room of the duplex Gilda and I shared with the beagle Petey and Petey's human family.

"Good evening," I improvised.

The sisters conveyed their disapproval of me, my greetings, my attitude and my right to be in the hereafter without saying a word or permitting a ripple to disturb the clouds of ashes that covered each one, from head to toe, hiding their faces.

Petey was stretched under the tree, her head between her paws, the most patient and welcoming entity on two planes of being, but she clearly wanted these strange gray critters who had invaded her home to go away. Lest I misread the intensity of Petey's feelings, she curled her upper lip and gave a flash of fangs.

If Petey is unhappy, I don't need anything more to be called to action.

"It was so nice of you to drop by." I spread my arms as though embracing the entire noiseless, grim assembly. "But that rascally old sun is creeping up the horizon again. I know you'll want to get back to your tunnel before photons get loose in the neighborhood. Bad photons, yucky photons."

As diplomatic suggestions go, this one needed a banged fist for anyone to pay attention. Time to unleash my inner wraith. The Somber Sisters could be as depressed as they liked, but they didn't have the right to suck the *joie de mort* from everyone else's afterlife. If they didn't want to smell the roses, they should keep their noses in the dirt.

Fortunately for the Somber Sisters, the ones nearest the dining room were already edging apart to admit Gilda to the discussion. She was still dressed in that silly blue Pollyanna dress and apron, and the smile that flickered across her face looked painful to produce.

"Isn't he so sweet, so thoughtful, so caring," Gilda said.

"Yes, aren't I just?" I muttered.

"I know you'll excuse him – that's so much like you – for not knowing about your problem," she told the assembled sisterhood. "Or not remembering my invitation to have you spend the day in our pots. We have dozens of them on the wall, as you can see."

Was it my imagination or had Gilda found a way to make the old coffeepots sparkle with a welcoming warmth? Were the Christmas tree lights glowing a little brighter? And had Petey been freshly bathed and combed?

"What's this about *their* problem?" I hissed. "And what gives you the right to invite them into our home?"

"You're just being fussy," Gilda said to me, while to the Somber Sisters she added: "He's so close to transcendence, he's about to pop out of his ectoplasm."

At the *T* word, the Somber Sisters flinched away from me. You'd've thought I was carrying the spectral version of cooties. They scurried past Gilda into the dining room and hopped into the plainest pot on the wall, the one with the handle taken from a mop with the dings and dents marking it as a former hobo's prized possession. And a certain ambience that should have informed the newcomers that it was my pot.

Gilda blocked me from chasing them out of my hobo coffeepot. "Those poor dears. Someone broke into the tunnel where they stay and left a mess. They won't be able to go back until the cleaners have been through the place."

"It looked alright"— I hastened not to add, *when I was there*, saying instead – "I mean, it looks alright to me to have them here."

She crossed her arms over her chest and gave me a slant-eyed appraisal. "Aren't you the sweetest, most considerate, most gentlemanly entity I've ever met? I can't imagine how I ever got a different impression of you."

"What impression was that?"

A cloud swept over a face that now had purple lips, eye shadow applied heavily enough to camouflage an infantry platoon, and iceberg-white makeup.

"I can't say," she said. "In fact, I can't remember how you used to be. I just know you were different before."

I glanced at Petey. *Go ahead, I'm not listening*, Petey seemed to say with a flick of her flappy ears. She rolled onto a side to face the tree.

"You can stop pretending to be Pollyanna now." I even tried to huff in exasperation, although it came off as a soft *blat*. "You've got the part, you're in the play. Just drop the act for now."

Gilda's eyes widened into saucers. Did I suddenly look even more peculiar than the Somber Sisters? She said, "This is not an act. This is my new paranormal."

"What are the Goths of the afterlife going to say? How will other spooks react when they look at you for the Gothic input on issues?"

"They'll just have to learn to look at me when they want a smile and a cheery word."

I groaned. "I was counting on you, Gilda."

"And you still can." She leaned closer, smiling. "Only now, I'm bringing a spoonful of sugar."

Twenty-one

CHAPTER

Spooks aren't supposed to dream. Nor do we wander around unconsciously after we've turned into a puddle of ectoplasm. I mean, would you want to admit to your friends that you've been *walking in your despecterization?* That sounds so silly that everyone avoids doing it.

Anyway, getting back to dreams, which we don't do, except for those times that we do, I seem to have had one of those can-do moments a few hours later while I was a glob of pure ectoplasm on the bottom of an early American coffeepot.

Here's what I dreamt: A breeze was coming off the river, punctuated by puffs of wind that stirred the bushes and rattled the overhead stoplights at the intersections. The city slept under a fluffy blanket and, as happened to me when I escaped from the Yankee invasion of the hotel basement, the air glittered with crystalline husks of snowflakes swirling through the darkness, unwilling to commit themselves to a quiet rest upon the earth.

I was among them now, no greater and no lesser than any other snowflake, a spark of animation upon the night, a moment of precision and beauty before the shadow consumes all. And I wanted to carry this feeling – this conviction, this joy for lightness and the dance – throughout my remaining postmortal existence. A great lesson was borne upon the darkness and sharing it with my friends in Specters Anonymous would be the best gift I could give them.

My hand stretched out like a child reaching into a jar filled with fireflies. And, there, I have it! Yet when I pulled my hand from the jar and unclenched my fingers, nothing was there.

Time to leave. Let's go. Get a move on.

Shaking off the dream, I returned to my posthumous essence at the bottom of a collector's coffeepot on a shelf in central Virginia. *I was I*, as a minor poet once observed, *And nothing else remained to do / But begin the game anew.*

In this case, the game was already underway. Somber Sisters streamed at a steady, unhurried pace from my beloved hobo coffeepot. Gilda was bathed in an aura of goodwill and relaxed competence as she poked her head down the spouts of other containers and exhorted their occupants to pull themselves together and get moving.

I snagged her before she could check a sharp-angled Art Deco pot that used to be her favorite. "What's going on?"

"We've got to evacuate the house. Everyone must move quickly and quietly toward the west."

"But we're spooks. What could possibly hurt us?"

Gilda had an answer in two syllables, although she needed four syllables to properly express herself: "Yaaan-Keees."

PETEY, THE BEAGLE who ran this house, squatted by the coffee table in the living room as specters left the safety of their pots and drifted through the walls.

I glided toward her and lowered myself until only my head and shoulders stuck out from the carpet. Petey would typically roll on her side to invite an astral massage whenever I got this close, but tonight she didn't move.

"Something's on your mind, girl. Are you worried about Yankees too?"

Petey's chocolaty eyes radiated a thoughtful warmth. Her upper lip rippled. I sensed a struggle taking place along her neurons as she tried to change *Ruff, ruff, RUFF* into *Here's what I think of the situation, old bean.*

Popping up to peek through the front window, I saw about fifty spooks in spectral blue lined on the street in front of our duplex. An officer at the head of the ranks shouted and slashed the air with his ectoplasmic sword.

I dropped to the carpet again. "Why us? Why are we getting attacked? What makes us different from any other house in the neighborhood?"

Petey glanced at the Christmas tree. At the plastic figure of a soldier in desert fatigues who rocked gently at the end of a bough.

Dawkins! The Yankees probably think we're holding him hostage.

Descending through the carpet until my nose brushed Petey's, I said, "Delay them for as long as you can. Then run upstairs. You have my permission to get on the big bed."

With such a deal, Petey sprang to her feet while I went in the other direction. Gilda was no longer in the dining room, and I didn't bother to check whether any spooks were left in the coffeepot collection. She may look like Pollyanna, but she still had a Goth's eye for details.

The western sky was a bruised purple when I dashed down the side of the hill. Hank had converted some of his ectoplasm into a muzzleloader and ammunition pouch. As he popped a glistening droplet of ectoplasm into the barrel, the Somber Sisters lined up between him and the hillside.

Lined up doesn't quite set the scene. Imagine this: Start with a pile of ashes about the size of an average spook. Then press it shoulder-to-shoulder against five or six other ash heaps, each the dimensions of a standard Somber Sisters. Then take more spook-sized ashes, and stack them on top of each other, four or five sisters high. Forming an inhuman shield between Hank and the Yankees' most likely avenue of attack.

I gotta hand it to the sisters. When it comes to upholding their pacifist beliefs, they'll go down swinging.

Gilda glowed. "Isn't it thrilling to see spooks so committed to nonviolence?"

"It'd feel better if the Yankees shared those feelings."

"I can hold them off a few minutes." Hank jabbed his ramrod into the ground. "That'll buy some time to get the civilians out of here."

"You don't have to do this," I said.

"Are you saying I can't do it?" Hank tightened his lips. His pigtail, nodded in agreement.

An ectoplasmic bullet hitting a spectral entity won't kill or maim, but it won't be pleasant either. Think of being trapped in a room whose floor, ceiling and walls were made entirely of blackboards that a million fingernails were scraping against.

"If you see a slouching fellow who looks like he hasn't shaken the dirt off his uniform in a century or so," I said, "give him special attention."

"With your compliments." Hank polished his front sight with his thumb and lifted the rifle to his shoulder.

With some tactful prodding by Gilda, the Somber Sisters accepted that greater challenges to their pacifism lay elsewhere. She and I led the sisters away, picking up a handful of puzzled spooks near Gillies Creek who wanted to know why the July 4th celebration was being held so early this year.

Slipping around the eastern slope of Libby Hill, we soon reached Church Hill and angled upward to the chapel that was home for the St. Sears group of Specters Anonymous. Our meeting wasn't scheduled for several hours, so instead of going to the room in the basement, I brought the group upstairs.

About half of the security lights were off, the rest dimmed, making the photon level tolerable for those of us on the spectral plane and leading me to wonder again whether Father Jenkins knew about the spooks who visited his church after the sun went down.

A few specters in the back pews was what I'd expect at this time of night, usually newbies waiting for an angelic concierge to show up with room assignments, but tonight the place was packed. Spooks were crammed together so tightly that even a miracle couldn't squeeze a hymnal between them.

"What gives?" I asked the first spook I knew, who happened to be Jingle Jim.

I could tell by his smirk that he'd been waiting all evening for someone to ask. He took a firm, declamatory stance and said: "Listen closely and you shall hear / A rattling sound / Drawing near. / It's astral knees aknocking in fear / For being on a battling ground."

"Feeling better now?" I asked.

He smiled. "I knew that you knowed / I was about to explode."

"If everyone else is having a painful night, why should the English language get off any easier?"

The Somber Sisters found places along the walls among followers of John the Plain in their simple white smocks and Newer-Age believers wearing astral track suits with stripes down the trousers and sleeves. Pressed into the aisles were Hindu spirits decked out in spectral loin cloths, plus Univisionists, Pragmatarians and some agnostics who came only partly through the church walls, still intent on keeping their options open.

Gilda eyed the crowd closely. My mind, with no conscious effort on its part, switched into snark mode and began sifting through my vast inventory of inappropriate remarks. The leading quip was: *The way you're studying those spooks, I'll bet there's a pop quiz coming that nobody told them about*, but something about her suggested that she was beyond appreciating my witticisms.

Put my perception down to the way her spectral form grew blurry, as though she were merely a distant image drifting in and out of focus, some moments a pert figure in an ordinary blue dress and starched apron, other times on the verge of respecterizing in her leather jacket, black tights and Gothic makeup.

"Do you ever wonder," she said so softly that she might have been talking to herself, "why so many spooks have no trouble finding their Uber-Spirit?"

"You mean, what did they figure out that we haven't?"

She shook her head. "No, it's more like: *What have they been through that I missed.*"

"Does the choice of an Uber-Spirit come down to that? Something that happens to us, not something we choose?"

She shrugged, and for once her shrug wasn't laden with nuance. "Maybe that's it. Or maybe it's a question of noticing something that's been in front of us all along."

"If that's the case, then there's no problem. We just gotta start paying attention."

She spun on me so fast I'd've thought she just realized a formerly testosterone-carrying target was within range. "It's easy for you to talk about having no problems. When things are going too well for you, you just go off and manufacture another crisis."

"What are you talking about?"

"Your transcendence," she shot back. "Your DVD at Margie's. All you've got to do is work a half-minute visit into your busy schedule, and you're out of here. Off you go to whatever comes after this place."

"But — "

"If you tell me one more time how rough your afterlife is, I'm going to get ugly."

For a flicker, she was Gilda the Goth, an astral bundle of black leather, clinky chains, bone-white skin, purple lips, purple fingernails, and a take-no-prisoners attitude. And this was before she lost her temper.

CHAPTER
Twenty-two

No one can get under my ectoplasm faster than Gilda. She can plant a doubt, give it some gentle nurturing, then kick-start it into action before I remember that I'd be safer sitting on the rim of an active volcano.

In the grand scheme of things, would it really matter whether spooks five years from now find roles in a holiday play on campus? Can I reasonably expect that even next year someone would remember a spook named Ralph who decided to add a spectral dimension to Dickens's *A Christmas Carol*?

Was I truly leaving a legacy? Or looking for reasons to delay crossing the next big abyss? At this crucial moment, a voice drifted between me and any danger of lapsing into meaningful self-analysis.

"But doesn't our literature say that we no longer try to avoid *the me-isms, photons and electrical appliances* that once threatened our transcendence?"

The voice was Mary Beth's, the newbie who had the misfortune to lead the meeting a few nights ago where the Somber Sisters showed up. The key phrase was from the *Teeny Book* of Specters Anonymous, and they came out in italics even when spoken.

"Define *avoid*," said another voice I recognized as Cal's, my sponsor.

"*Staying away from*," Mary Beth answered.

"Isn't that the same thing as running away?" I could imagine Cal crossing his arms over his chest as he said, "Regardless, I'm not convinced that *charging ahead* is a good idea."

"I couldn't agree with you more." The relief in Mary Beth's voice was clear.

This conversation took place in the choir loft of the packed church. Cal and Mary Beth had been joined by the Mahareshrash from the Hindu delegation to Specters Anonymous, John the Plain, Shepherd Sam, the ever-flamboyant

Jumpin' Jeffrey and other spooks I'd seen before but couldn't put a name to, all leaders of Richmond's 12-step groups for posthumous recovery.

Shepherd Sam sucked in his lower lip, and Cal seemed to lose interest in continuing this discussion. Mary Beth gave a great sigh of relief from her sanctuary in the shadows of the organ.

Sam had gone through the afterlife with eyes locked in a permanent squint, although he's usually the last one to worry about anything, including a sudden rush of photons. Perhaps he'd seen so much during his first life that the spiritual realm couldn't hold his attention for long.

"Let's put the philosophizing aside for a moment," he said with his slight Texas twang. "This church is overflowing with spooks who don't want to get caught between two spectral armies that're still working out their differences."

"So we should become a third army." Mary Beth, alarmed, didn't make it a question. Nor did she make it a statement that she was willing to stand behind.

Shepherd Sam hadn't developed his famous squint by looking away when trouble swaggered into the room. "This church is full of spooks who don't want any part of a fight. We should respect their wishes. Give them a safe place to stay until the dust settles."

" – As it were," I couldn't stop myself from adding.

Cal and Mary Beth shot me looks I would've preferred they kept to themselves. Shepherd Sam tightened his squint in my direction.

"Just the spook we need to talk to," Cal said.

I spun around to see who was behind me.

"Tomorrow night, this church will be lit up like a sparkler," Cal continued. "The Breathers will be busy with their church services. We can't expect our fellow spooks to be comfortable once the lights are turned on."

The left eyebrow on the Mahareshrash's serene face twitched, which translated in any of the major western languages into a scream of protest. If Cal or anyone else was going to volunteer the Mahareshrash's temple as a hideaway for a mob, they were going to learn that not everyone who once lived east of Suez is calm and inscrutable.

Shepherd Sam's squinty gaze didn't miss a thing. He saw where Cal was heading. "Half the area's deceased population is going to be attending Ralph's play tomorrow. We might as well invite the other half to join them."

"The convention center is bigger," I said.

"They're hosting the Annual Peace on Earth Car and Boat Show," Mary Beth said. "Too many photons there."

"But the theater isn't always dark," I protested. "The lights are on before the play. And at intermission. Then at the end."

"I'm sure our friends won't mind a little night air from time to time." Cal said.

Sam's squint tightened, his lips pursed, his chin dropped, and since none of the other spooks in the choir loft could think of anything to say, the meeting broke up and everyone drifted back into the melee in the pews. I could think of a couple of topics they might be interested in, especially the one about the play being canceled because of legal hitches, but Cal was soon the only spook hanging around, and I'd learned from long trial and error that Cal wasn't fond of any sentence that began with the word *but*.

He joined me near the ceiling as a second layer of spooks filled the area above the pews, and specters began spreading across the church on a third level. Cal crossed his arms over his chest and looked at me with the strangest expression. Almost a wince, although it widened his eyes.

"What are you doing with your face?" I asked.

"Smiling," Cal answered with Cal-like composure. "I'm very proud of you. Because of what you're doing with the play. Bringing some pleasure into the afterlives of your brethren — "

" — and sistren — "

" — spooks. And now you're going to make sure that our newbies have a safe place to stay tomorrow night, even if it's only for a few hours." Cal actually rocked back and forth on his heels; I still wasn't convinced he was free of pain. He added: "Way to go, Ralph."

"Yeah, I'm quite a guy."

"I hope you won't forget your friends back here after you transcend."

"It'll be tough, but I'll remember the little spooks."

Among the gazillions of ways that words can be put together, I was stumbling toward combinations that were guaranteed to pop my sponsor's bubble of serenity. Time to change the subject and let someone else break the bad news about the play's cancelation.

"What's with the spooks in blue coats patrolling our neighborhoods?" I asked. "The last time they tried, we had the famous Battle of Libby Hill. Is the Colonel losing his nerve?"

"It's not nerve the Colonel's losing, but troops. A few rebel outfits disappeared during the last couple nights. I don't think the Colonel could keep the Yankees out if he tried."

"How do you misplace a regiment in the afterlife?"

Cal eyed me with a squint he must've borrowed from Shepherd Sam. "They might have wandered off without telling anyone where they're going. Or they might have all transcended together."

I scratched my hairless astral chin. "How can that happen? Transcendence is a personal thing. What are the odds that a group of spooks would need to learn the same lesson, then pick it up at the same time?"

"About as remote as the chances I gave you for sticking with any 12-step program when we first met." Cal did that wincey thing again with his mouth.

I responded with my own wincey thing.

I WAS HALFWAY to the church ceiling and working out my next steps as more spooks took their places below and a snowflake buzzed me like a hungry white mosquito. I took a swing, the snowflake dodged the blow, and Hank respecterized where the snowflake had been.

"Alpha Patrol reporting in, boss," he said.

"What happened to the Yankees?" I asked. "I'm impressed you could delay them so long from chasing us down that hill."

"They're still on the top of that hill. I think they gotta do an environmental impact study before they can attack down an undeveloped slope."

"War ain't for the likes of us." I had been about to say, *for the faint of heart*, but being spooks, we're technically heartless, so faintness isn't a factor.

"Amen," he said.

Like the slow roll of distant thunder, another long, jagged "Amen" boomed from the spooks stretched over the pews.

I leaned closer to Hank. "Once this crowd realizes that no archangels are coming to hand out wings, they'll get restless. Why don't you continue our auditions for the play?"

"Only got two or three parts to fill," Hank said.

"When you finish that, start the rehearsals. Right here. The crowd might enjoy watching."

Hank eyed the spooks jostling for space on the third spectral row, with a steady flow of anxious spirits streaming through the walls, ceiling and floor.

"Prepare to be awed," he whispered to the crowd.

If the pigtail at the back of his head could talk, I'm sure it would add, *And sit up straight and stop fidgeting.*

MY NEXT MOVE was to check with Margie's effort to get legal protection for the fraternity that was putting on the play.

Her psychic parlor was a nanosecond or two away from the church. Gilda was already in the waiting room in full Pollyanna array, complete with an optimistic smile and hands folded placidly on her lap.

"Shouldn't you be in the church with everyone else?" I said.

She didn't move, though I sensed a subtle change. Not in her, but in the room. It seemed to have gotten chilly.

"I wouldn't dare to actually suggest you need to be there," I stammered. "Or tell you to go anywhere else."

She worked a wrinkle from her apron. "I thought I could be of best service to you here."

This new, improved Gilda, mild-mannered, soft-spoken and always looking on the bright side of the lilies, was a strange creature. Only a few nights ago, I wouldn't have hesitated to drive her out of the room with an appropriately inappropriate remark for the sheer sport of the challenge. Now that felt cheap.

What was going on with me? Have I become afraid of hurting her feelings? Was I beginning to enjoy the updated version of Gilda? Or, lest I be accused of conduct unbecoming for the hereafter's leading cynic, was I treating this new apparition gingerly until I figured out the best way to unsettle her?

Beats me. I'm brain-dead. What do I know?

"How's our friend Esmerelda doing?" she asked.

Even in Pollyanna mode, Gilda could stop me cold.

"Dunno. Last time I saw her, she was riding off with a bunch from Heck's Angels."

"I'm so sorry." Gilda flashed an ever-optimistic smile. "I know it must be weighing on your mind."

"A weight. Yes."

"Wait?" The word exploded from a Breather in the waiting room, an old duffer sitting on a chrome and plastic sofa. A younger man beside him reached over to pat his hand. I tagged them as a worn-out adult son and his dottering, gray-haired father. The older gent startled me with that apt remark, although, of course, he wasn't aware that Gilda and I were there.

Or was he?

"I don't know how much longer I can wait," the old-timer told his son. "Not while the streets are crawling with those . . . those things. We've got to keep moving. They're getting closer. I can feel it."

Through the bay window overlooking the street, I saw a dark shadow drift across the snow-covered lawns. Another Yankee patrol winding through the heart of the Confederate capital. Cautious, stealthy, unopposed.

"Don't they look quite handsome?" Gilda said, beside me now. "I know they're supposed to be the enemy. But that shouldn't stop us from appreciating their finer qualities."

"Is that why you're here? To help me deal with that army?"

"Gracious, no." Gilda clutched her hands to her breast as though I was the silliest entity she'd ever met. "You can deal with an army better than any spook I know."

"Nice of you to say that."

"It's the man down the hall with Margie. He's the one you're going to need help with."

Twenty-three

CHAPTER

awyer Stuart Q. Stewart had arranged himself on one side of the table in Margie's consulting room as though he intended to stay, leaving Margie wedged into a corner by the table with the fishbowl that served as her crystal ball.

On most faces, I'd describe Margie's look as a silent plea for help, but Gilda, Veronica and Rosetta had taught me that any ideas I have about their vulnerability were actually signs of my own immaturity.

"I'd be honored to represent the fraternity if it's sued," lawyer Stewart said. "Contingent upon their ability to provide a meaningful retainer. And let's not forget ongoing expenses. Plus, I'd want proof of sufficient monetary resources to mount a legal defense."

"I see." Margie had a dazed expression.

The lone occupant of the fishbowl pressed its face to the glass for a better look at Stewart. Then me. Wagging its head, the fish swam behind a porcelain shipwreck.

For someone with a heartbeat, lawyer Stewart had spent a lot of time on the fringes of my afterlife. He was landlord to Big G's detective agency, the attorney who handled the last will of Margie's ex-partner, and now the legal adviser to Margie ever since she inherited a few pieces of property.

The fact that Stewart was a genuine, respiring, hormone-equipped male had nothing to do with my attitude toward the fellow. Not the slightest effect whatsoever. Zip, zilch, nada.

"Isn't it amazing how he manages to remember so much?" Gilda whispered. "If I had that much information in my head, it'd get all mashed together. The whereas's would be wrapped around the forsooths. I wouldn't be able to tell my habeas corpus from Mrs. Hannity's."

"Yeah, I have that problem with her too," I quipped.

Stewart pulled a brown leather attache case from the floor, clicked open the lid and rooted through the contents, which, from my angle, consisted mostly of frayed paperback novels and old newspapers, exactly the contents I'd expect from a lawyer so desperate for business that he'll make house calls in the middle of the night.

Margie finally lost her patience and didn't seem willing to waste another second waiting for it to wander back. "I've already taken too much of your time."

"No trouble at all. Let me just show you my sample contract." Laying a folder on Margie's side of the table, he pulled out paperclipped papers and tapped the top page. "It's all there. On the bottom you'll notice a few pages with frequently asked questions."

Margie gave Stewart a pained smile. "I wish my friend who recommended you was around to see this."

Gilda took the hint before I realized Margie was talking about me. "Let me take a look at it," Gilda said. She glided through the table and the fishbowl and settled behind Margie's shoulder, as the lawyer leaned back in his chair, smug, comfortable, pleased with both his performance and the audience. Shakespeare showing his latest sonnet to a fan couldn't've had more pride of authorship.

The sleeve of his suit coat rode up his arm to expose the face of his wristwatch. That's where Spunky came in, the wraith who haunts the world's smaller digital appliances.

Spunky was dressed for the season. His nose was as red as a feverish cherry, tiny wings sprouted from the sides of his head, and miniature Christmas tree ornaments hung from his hair, ears and eyebrows.

A blissful look clouded his eyes as he said, "When what to my ectoplasmic eyes did appear / But a sled pulled by wraiths, and not by reindeer."

I groaned.

"Can't you just picture it, boss." Spunky was so excited, the ornaments in his hair began to tinkle. "The theater is quiet. The lights are out. All eyes are on the stage. Then from every seat in the place – from every digital watch, cell phone, pager, iPad and pacemaker – this cheery face pops out, singing *Spunky, the Frosted Wraith*."

"Wonderful, just wonderful," I muttered. "But you know, Hank is handling auditions. You'll have to take this up with him."

Without another word, Spunky sank into Stewart's watch as the glowing tip of his nose darkened.

Gilda peered over Margie's shoulder at Stewart's contract on the table. She whispered, "I think you've got his hopes up. Time now to mention the magic word — *insurance*."

"I don't think Spunky can do any damage," I answered.

"We're not talking to you," Gilda and Margie said in unison.

"I didn't think you were," said Stewart, flinching away, unaware of Gilda or me. "But who would you be talking to, then?"

Margie brushed away Gilda's spectral finger to point at the contract. "It says here you'll help with insurance claims. Is that life insurance or car insurance?"

"Liability insurance." Stewart spread his hands to indicate a subject too vast for a layperson to grasp. "Insurance can cover damages for all sorts of things. Hollywood used to insure the legs of famous dancers from injury. Or the voices of singers. There's insurance if you lose your laptop, break the glass on your cell phone or become too sick to take a scheduled vacation."

"How about insurance if someone gets hurt in a theater you're renting?" Margie asked.

Stewart shuddered. Like a fisherman touching an electric eel. Or a struggling businessman watching his fee sink from reach.

"Sure," he said. "That might work. I guess so."

"Wouldn't getting insurance be simpler and cheaper than all this?" she said, hoisting the lawyer's thick contract.

Stewart salvaged his composure in time to suggest that he might be able to come up with something more economical than his standard full-services contract, something that would beat the best liability insurance. As he rummaged through the paperbacks and old newspapers in his attache case for the right form, Margie excused herself to check on her next client. Gilda followed her into the hall, with me in the rear.

"That wasn't too difficult," Margie told Gilda.

Gilda curtsied. "I am in the presence of a master at wrapping a flimflam artist in his own web."

They probably would've locked arms and skipped into the kitchen to share cookies and milk if Margie hadn't noticed me in the hallway.

"As for you," she said, "I'll contact the frat house to let them know they're covered if they run into legal troubles."

I glanced down her narrow, dark hallway. To the door that led to her private apartment. Where a DVD player shared a homemade wooden stand with a stereo and a television set. Somewhere in the room, perhaps stuffed between sofa cushions or serving as a coaster for a pot of ferns, was a plastic box marked *The Honeymooners.*

"Your last disc is already in the machine," Margie said. "It'll just take a second to turn it on. I'll leave you in peace while I say good-bye to the lawyer."

Not even I could kid myself any more. My work here was done: Hank was rehearsing the spooks who would make a spectral contribution to *A Christmas Carol*: The curtain would rise on opening night without me. Nothing stood between me and my final, pretranscendence lesson except a single door that I could float through like an elephant through a spider web.

Gilda nudged me with an elbow, careful not to wrinkle her Pollyanna apron. She knew what was tumbling through my mind.

"I can go with you, if you like." She was earnest in a way that only Pollyanna can be. "I'm sure Margie would be happy to join us."

"It would be an honor," Margie replied.

Something strange was happening in the interior recesses that pass for my brain. A dissolving and a reshaping, and I could almost feel my ectoplasm slide through that door. Nearly, but not quite, for an awareness of danger is one of the few things we carry with us from the cemetery. I had to look over my shoulder.

At the other end of the hall, the twinkling holiday lights on the bay window sprayed colorful dots through the waiting room. A dark form moved across the door frame. Spectral in nature, its body layered in ashen shadows suggestive of a military uniform, but without any detail, his head made of angles and flat surfaces.

"Dawkins!"

I was after him faster than a mosquito can spit.

Dawkins must not have known that spooks leave a slight disturbance on the astral plane that can be tracked by another spirit, especially one with a postnatural aptitude for such things and training at Big G's detective agency. For me, following Dawkins was as easy as a Breather stalking muddy footprints across a kitchen floor.

He went due south until he reached the James, then cruised downriver toward the business district, stopping several times to board spectral ships hundreds of feet above the water that were making their way inland.

(Note to readers: Do you think of The Flying Dutchman *when you imagine spooks at sea? A battered wreck with breached planks in the hull and sails torn into rags, wandering the seven seas without a crew. Once again, Hollywood has gotten the afterlife all wrong. Picture, instead, a tall-masted schooner, with a full complement of spooks*

tending the sails, repairing the ropes, scrubbing the decks. Then take away the ship, sails, ropes and decks without disturbing the spectral crew hustling about their nightly chores. What's left is an authentic ghost ship.)

Dawkins visited each vessel briefly, although in one case crewmen with ectoplasmic cutlasses kept him from boarding. When he was directly above a collection of rocks, sand and scrub brush known as Belle Island, he descended.

I waited as he faded into the thicket in the center of the island before lowering myself near the shoreline. Splintered plywood and tar paper scraps marked the remnants of a shack hammered together by kids on summer vacation where I spent my first days in the afterlife in a discarded paint bucket.

I shook my head and glanced away. Even hovels deserve a monument.

The dim silvery edge of a large can peeked under a soggy cap that once had been a cardboard container for cheap wine. Could it be the very can in which my ectoplasm had puddled for weeks, safe from the rays of scavenging photons before I learned that I didn't have to go through the afterlife alone?

Confident I would recognize the pattern of cracks on the paint that had dried inside, I drifted closer. The tangy scent of a chemical cocktail wafted from the container. Wasn't that paint fleck lying on the rim the same shade of gray-lime-yellow? I eased forward, expectant, almost convinced I'd see my old self inside if I was quiet enough.

"If I knew you were coming, I'd've faked a wake."

The voice from the can wasn't mine. Thankfully. Nor were the eyes that careened in their sockets like sailors on a stormy deck.

"Is it time to get up already?" Esmee whined. "Feels like I just went to bed."

"You probably did."

Esmee trickled from the can and pulled herself together on the beach. A spook respecterizing from a puddle of ectoplasm can be a disorderly thing, especially one who, judging from her frazzled condition, must have spent hours sitting in a vat of embalming fluid at a local mortuary. But that didn't make sense. The last time I saw her, she was riding behind the Heck's Angel leader on a spectral Harley-Davidson.

"Where have you been?" I asked.

"After a little spin through the Shenandoah valley, my biker buddies dropped me off at the frat house."

"That can fluster the best of us."

"Did you know that one of those little rascals at the Alpha Beta Charlie . . . or whatever . . . collects butterflies?" she slurred. "He has these stinky vials in his room. Ever wonder where the word *vile* came from? Disgusting things, I can tell you." She paused. "Let's hurry before someone else finds them."

I grabbed her earlobe as she tried to glide away, an easier task than it'd usually be, seeing as how when she pulled herself together she forgot that ears go on heads, not feet.

"How about playing a game?" I asked.

"Great." She slapped me hard. "Tag! You're it."

Snickering and twittering, she darted away. I grabbed her ear again, which was now coming from her ankle.

"The game is going to be Cowboys and Indians. We're the Indians, and we're going to creep up on the cowboys and find out what they're up to."

"Goody." Esmee's eyeballs did a victory loop in their sockets. "I'll be the princess Hitahontas."

"What?"

"Swatahontas."

"I don't understand."

"Pocahontas."

"No one can do it better."

CHAPTER Twenty-four

here were only so many ways I could tell Esmerelda that she didn't know what Indian headdresses looked like. I have my limits for futile behavior. Besides, perhaps an actual tribe somewhere wore its feathers coming from ears and eyebrows.

As it turned out, Esmee and I didn't need camouflage to track Dawkins to his destination in the rocky interior of the island.

Belle Island was a prison camp during the war. *(Note to readers: If you have to ask* Which war? *you haven't been paying attention. Go back to page one and start over.)* The island's few acres were filled with spooks in blue still searching for their final resting places, as though that would solve any problems.

The farther Dawkins went into the island, the more Yankees gathered around him until he was completely surrounded and the only paths left were up and down, and even the vertical escape routes were filling up.

Dawkins acted as though this crowd didn't measure up to his usual standards, but he'd make the best of the situation anyway. "Listen up," he told the group. "I've got something you have to hear."

"Slow down, Mr. Dawkins." A blue-shirted spook shouldered his way through the crowd. It was Sarge, whom I met earlier by the war memorial. His eyes simmered with authority and his mouth didn't waste time smiling. "We've been over this before, and I'll only tell you one more time. In this outfit, only the commander makes assignments."

Dawkins could match Sarge on anyone's stern-o-meter. "Fair enough. Where's your commander?"

A flurry of whispers broke out among the Yankees. Sarge sidled closer to Dawkins, stretching his ectoplasmic form discreetly as he went so he and Dawkins ended up seeing things eye-to-eye.

"No one's seen the commander since shortly after your last visit," Sarge said. "You wouldn't happen to know what happened to him, would you?"

Dawkins wasn't used to answering questions. "Your commander isn't important any more. What I have to say – what you need to hear – *is* important."

"Troops, dis-MISSED."

Sarge snapped out the last syllable like a pistol going off in everyone's back pocket. Yankees despecterized so quickly that some left spots of blue behind. Not blue *on* anything. Just blue, all by its lonesome, too puzzled by its abandonment to know what to do next, so it just hung there.

Esmee wanted to improve her view and the best seat in the house seemed to be between Dawkins and Sarge. I dragged her back into the shadows, protesting all the way.

"You're no fun. Things are just getting interesting," she said. "This is what your dumb play lacks. Conflict, raised voices, thrown punches.

"We're residents of the spiritual plane," I protested. "We're supposed to have outlived punches."

"And you wonder why death has a bad reputation," she huffed.

For once I suppressed the first words about to roll off my tongue. Besides, *Oh yeah* wasn't my best comeback.

Sarge gave Dawkins a long, steady glare before easing away, just to make sure Dawkins understood that Sarge was backing away but not backing down. For a long time Dawkins stood motionless amid the scrub brush, his uniform caked with the dirt from two planes of existence.

I glided next to him. "It must be tough when not even your own people will listen to you."

Dawkins turned toward me with a face that could've been made with a wood chisel. "My people?"

"We don't care if the entire Yankee army is behind you. You're not going to stop our play. The show will go on."

Slowly, Dawkins shook his head. If he weren't already deceased, I'd've wondered if he was nodding off. "What makes you think I want to stop it?"

His eyes were (Dare I say it?) dead. They looked at me without quite focusing. As though I weren't worth the effort to see clearly.

"What I think isn't the issue," I said. "We're not going to let you sabotage the play."

That got his attention. "Is that all you think I'm doing?" he said.

"I don't care how many of your friends you bring or what you do or say. We are going ahead with the show."

Something about Dawkins nagged at me as I led Esmee from the island. We passed without incident to our duplex on Libby Hill, then through the living room to the collection of coffeepots on the dining room wall. Christmas lights glowed from the windows and the tree in the front room. I shoved Esmee into a formal English teapot on the dining room shelves. Sensing my mood, she went quietly.

For the next twelve hours I was going to be in my own bucket, with my beagle sleeping on the floor below, James William's family puttering about their daily routines, and Gilda and Esmee nearby in case I had a sudden urge to be agitated.

Not until I despecterized into a puddle of ectoplasm did the full weight of Dawkins's last words – "Is that *all* you think I'm doing?"– fully register. The spook admitted he'd been trying to ruin our play. But something else was going on, something larger than disrupting the holiday plans of Breathers and spooks alike.

I puddled into the bottom of the coffee can with the image of Dawkins's dazed, ashen face dissolving throughout my ectoplasm.

DEAD TO THE *world* may apply to some out-of-touch Sunshiners, but the world is never dead to us spooks. The holiday season is a time when bustle, excitement, hopes and goodwill can make even the grumpiest spirits pull themselves out of their buckets with an indefinable *something* coursing through whatever we've got left for coursing.

I heard Gilda's and Esmee's voices in the living room.

"No, no, dear," Gilda murmured. "I'm not sure that's where we belong. Why don't you come down, and we'll find someplace nicer."

"What could possibly be better than this?" Esmee said, sulking.

I rounded the corner into the living room and the discussion fell into place. Esmee was on top of the Christmas tree. Or, to be precise, on the tip of the uppermost plastic ray of the golden star that James William's family had crowned the tree with.

Esmee had a snowy robe whose sleeves and hem were embroidered, and a halo of twinkling lights in red, green, yellow and white encircled her head. The fingers of one of Esmee's spectral hands riffled a deck of cards, while the other rattled a pair of dice. Her mouth was occupied by a cigar large enough to make Big G jealous.

"Hiya, hiya, hiya," she said. "I am the Ghost of Christmas As It Might Be If You're Very, Very Lucky. Hiya, hiya, hiya."

Gilda dithered at the base of the tree in Pollyanna attire. "The poor dear heard me mention the Ghost of Christmas Present and thought I was talking about gifts."

"Make your own gifts. Think large," Esmee said from the top of the tree. "Hiya, hiya, hiya. Are you feeling lucky, sailor?"

I didn't put up with the indignities of a mortuary to go through this. "I'm feeling very lucky. But your luck is about to run out."

Exactly what I would do wasn't the issue. I'd figure it out in the fraction of a nanosecond that it took to get within snapping distance of Esmee's nose.

Instead, Gilda gripped my wrist. "You can be more helpful elsewhere."

"Getting Esmee off that tree is the perfectly – "

Before I got any further, Gilda's Pollyanna demeanor slipped, and I caught a glimpse of pure Goth. The kind of Goth who thought nail-studded cudgels were a conversation starter.

"Maybe I should check on Petey," I said.

"In the kitchen," Gilda said, not taking her eyes off Esmee.

"I was just heading there."

My favorite beagle, Petey, was stretched on the kitchen tiles. Petey's favorite pet, the boy James William, squirmed on a stool by the window. He breathed on the glass, giving it a misty glaze, then sketched on the surface.

"Billy Murphy's mother lets him open one present on Christmas Eve," James William said, doodling. His tone was so offhanded it was a wonder the poor lad didn't fall asleep right there on his stool.

His mother matched his indifference as she rinsed dishes in the sink and set them on a rack. "Perhaps you might want to have Christmas with the Murphys. If Santa can't find you there, I'm sure he'll make it up next year."

"If you let me open one present now, then Santa won't have to worry about finding me at the Murphys." James William eyed his mother carefully. "Isn't that being considerate of other people's feelings?"

"Nice try, tiger." Mother pushed the rack of plates into the dishwasher and closed its door. "I'll tell you what I will let you do. You can take any ornament from the tree that you like – even the soldier – and play with it until we go to the theater."

James William erased a tic-tac-toe game from the frosted window with a single swipe of his hand. "He left."

"Pardon?"

"He left. Private Dawkins who was guarding the tree. When I got up this morning, he was gone."

Mother dried her hands on a towel. "He must have fallen off his branch."

"Nope. I checked."

Mother glanced at Petey. Petey met her gaze evenly. He wouldn't take the rap for this. If he wanted to snatch ornaments off the tree, the candy canes would be history. He couldn't be distracted by plastic dolls.

"Well, your soldier certainly didn't walk away." Mother motioned for boy and beagle to follow her from the kitchen.

"Can so," James William said, although only Petey and I were there to hear that.

I joined the parade into the living room and watched as Mother shifted packages under the Christmas tree, looking for the tiny replica of a soldier in a desert camouflage uniform. Soon all the packages had been moved to the sofa, and by the time Hank arrived Mother and son were shaking bows and loosely taped parcels for the missing ornament.

"Let me guess," Hank said. "This is competitive gift wrapping."

"I don't supposed you've seen a soldier. About so tall and dressed for a week in the Sahara."

"No one that teeny," Hank said. "But you can't go five or six blocks tonight without bumping into another patrol. Some rebels, some bluecoats. And the amazing thing is that they never seem to run into each other."

"What are the odds of that happening," I mumbled to myself as I pictured Dawkins's troubled face last night. *Is that all you think I'm doing?*

Hank must've sensed I was about to say something meaningful, for he kicked the conversation into another direction.

"You can scratch our Number One casting problem from your to-do list."

"Which problem is that?"

"The one from the first act. When Scrooge returns home and the knocker on the front door turns into his dead partner."

"Are we overthinking this? Let's put a spook there, have him say the lines, and move on."

Hank eased aside to avoid slipping into Mother's left shoulder. "Let me show you what I've got in mind."

By now, Petey had joined Mother and James William, groping through the packages. To a beagle, if anyone spends so much time looking for something, there has to be food at the end of the search.

"We're going this way," Hank said.

His pigtail waved me to the foyer, and I passed through the front door, glided across the porch and down the stairs, and, at his direction, turned around halfway to the sidewalk. Okay, the door wasn't designed for drama, so I shouldn't be too critical, but isn't an outside door just a wood slab on a couple of hinges? As for knockers, this one had a brass ring the size of a half dollar. Purely decorative, not something that'd thunder through the house to announce a visitor. Once this knocker got down to business, it'd sound more like a spoon clinking against a teacup.

Hank's pigtail lifted in a request for silence. He said: "Shadows! Ectoplasm! INACTION!" Hank is aces with a lot of things, although he doesn't do subtle.

I'll give him credit, though. I knew something was going on with the knocker before I could say what it was. Like dawn on a winter's morning when even the sun isn't eager to get moving, the brass ring and its metal plate slowly brightened. By the time I could identify the color as a sort of phosphorescent green, the knocker was changing shape, getting longer, more three-dimensional, round in some places and stringy and frayed in others.

"I can see a face," I said. "And what's that? A funny hat? How does a funny hat fit into a Christmas story?"

"That's hair. It's called dreadlocks."

The face had a smile as long as a July afternoon and didn't belong in a ghost story. Or anywhere that searchlights figure into a list of things to avoid at all costs.

"Waz up, me mon?" said the face on the knocker. "We be having a par-TEE?"

I gave Hank a look. "He's supposed to be Marley's ghost."

"And he is. And I'm not talking about some puffed up, make-believe Marley. That's the actual ghost of Marley."

"But — "

"Bob Marley, the Jamaican singer."

"Let me have another look at the script."

Twenty-five

CHAPTER

After Hank left to let me think things over, I'm not sure how long I stayed outside the duplex on Libby Hill, staring at the Bob Marley door knocker that stared back at me, wondering whether it's a good sign or a bad one that the afterlife has gone from strange to kooky. Whether this was the moment to dig in my heels and insist upon a semblance of order within the paranormal. Or whether it was time to move on.

"Do you know that your mouth is open?" Gilda said when she arrived.

As a favor, I swung my lower jaw closed.

"What are you watching?" she asked.

I nodded at the front door. Where Marley's ghost had, of course, disappeared.

"Oh," she said.

She stood next to me, our shoulders brushed, our eyes locked on the front of the house. Overhead, a canopy of clouds squeezed the last vestiges of daylight from the sky. A few snowflakes the size of oak leaves floated to the ground.

I eyed her carefully. "Do you think it would do me any good to get in touch with my inner Pollyanna?"

"Only if you've got one. Which I doubt."

"What do I have?"

Gilda didn't have to think long. "You've got an inner Peter Pan."

I let the idea settle on me as casually as the large snowflakes drifted toward the lightly dusted ground. That might explain everything. Instead of Wendy, I had Gilda. Substitute Petey for Nana. For the Lost Boys, there's Hank and the gang.

But who's my Captain Hook? Dawkins comes quickly to mind, but he's only been around the last couple nights. Maybe the absence of a Captain Hook in my afterlife means I'm in better shape than Peter Pan was. Or maybe it means my personal Captain Hook will come swaggering around the corner at any moment.

I turned to Gilda.

Before I could open my mouth, she said, "You're thinking too much again."

She checked the knot of her apron in back and puffed at a snowflake that was drifting toward the cuff of her immaculate blouse. The snowflake was unmoved.

"I wonder what Cal would say?" I asked.

"Do the next *left* thing," she answered without hesitation. "What's the most important thing left for you to do?"

We both knew that question led back to Margie's and the DVD player ready to roll with the last few seconds of *The Honeymooners* and the missing lesson that would launch my transcendence out of here.

Thankfully, at that moment, a little pandemonium began to jell. From a corner of my eye, I saw a rumpled dark blue cap poke above the guardrail at the end of the street, followed by the rest of a Yankee's head, bug-eyed and intent, staring past Gilda and me. In the other direction, toward the Confederate monument, a patrol of rebel spooks was gliding stealthily our way, ectoplasmic rifles at the ready.

Gilda nudged me toward the porch. We were familiar with the Southern tradition of shooting first and leaving before it was time for questions. The rebels crept closer. If the Confederate boys had working glands they'd be salivating from hopes that Gilda or I would make a sudden move that justified a bayonet charge.

So intense were they that they didn't miss a step when Bob Marley reappeared on the door knocker and said, "Dis be da par-TEE? Mighty sad peeble to be friends wid, mon."

The Confederate patrol inched toward us; Gilda struggled to suppress her inner Goth. I saw flashes of black leather trying to replace a starched apron; purple fingernails clawing from the tips of her freshly scrubbed hands; and a smile that was striving mightily not to yield to a snarl.

Esmee flew through the living room window in a football uniform and puffy pink slippers. "Stand aside, kids. I'll protect you."

A glance at Esmee brought Gilda back to her Pollyanna senses.

"That's so thoughtful of you, Miz Esmerelda," Gilda said. "But I believe we have the situation under control."

In fact, that was the case, although none of us could claim credit. The Union spooks who'd been peeking over the guardrail at the end of the block were gone, and the rebel patrol that'd been nearing them reversed course without, apparently, ever noticing them.

I looked at Gilda. "The next left thing, huh?"

AFTER RESPECTERIZING a few miles away in the walk-in freezer of a Richmond grocery store, I worked my way down an aisle of vegetables and fruit to the back wall that loomed in the dim light like the side of an iceberg.

The next left thing would have to wait while I checked the produce section.

Private Carson squatted in a corner where streams of chilly air flowed into the freezer from vents near the floor. I've always meant to ask how he managed to smuggle horn-rimmed glasses into the hereafter. Everything about the pudgy spook was due for a do-over. His uniform was wrinkled, his hair rumpled, his posture wretched and his attitude rebellious. For reasons that defy understanding, even on my side of the daisies, the Colonel trusted Carson to run his intelligence center.

"Have I asked if you've got any information about a spook named Dawkins?" I asked.

"Nope."

Carson wore an expression that reminded me of a newly deceased physics professor who once tried to convince me that death was simply the space-time continuum being doubled back on itself and stapled.

"The answer is *No* to the question of whether I'd asked before," I muttered to myself. "So let me ask now whether you have information about Dawkins?"

"I do."

Carson's face was a model of sincere helpfulness. I fought to keep my astral presence from turning beet red. "Things are narrowing down nicely. What can you tell me about Dawkins?"

Carson's attention strayed to the stream of cold air rippling through the vents with misty text, mainly with five or six columns of letters and numbers, lined neatly side-by-side.

He struggled to conceal a mischievous grin. *Never trust anyone who looks at numbers with a twinkle in his eye,* said Fast Eddie, who knows about such things. *That twinkle means they see things you're going to regret.*

"First name?" he asked.

"Private."

Carson's mouth did a reasonable imitation of a guppy trying to suck in water. I lifted a warning finger. "If you give me more narrow answers to broad questions, I may do things I'll later be sorry for."

"We can't have that," Carson said, his twinkle growing stronger.

"Tell me everything you know about a Yankee private named Dawkins."

"Nothing to tell. No Union spooks by that name around here."

"And you would know?"

Carson lifted his hand next to the fog with its rows of data shooting up from the vent. If he were dealing with something other than chilled air, I'm sure he'd give it a comforting pat.

"Since the Yankees don't have a Private Dawkins, then he's got to come from" – I relaxed whatever passes for my mind and cleared the way to blurt out the first random thought that struggled its way to the finish line – "the rebel forces."

Carson sagged. Suddenly this game wasn't any fun.

"So Dawkins is in a Confederate outfit?" I asked.

He shook his head. "No."

"And you would know if he was?"

He nodded.

Even by the standards of Carson's world, this was getting bizarre.

"But you said you had information about Dawkins. Who is he? What's he up to? Who's he working with?"

He turned away and swirled a hand through the mist rising from the vent. "What I have about Dawkins is where he's been."

"That's not going to tell me anything." The trace of a smoldering twinkle was kindled in Carson's eyes, and I hastened to add: "Is it?"

The columns of text disappeared from the stream of chilled air spurting from the vent, replaced by a map of Richmond dotted with X's and O's and arrows and lines and even, in one corner, a miniature raven – all graphic representations of the tactical deployment of forces throughout the city.

"I don't see – " I started to say.

Carson hoisted a cautionary finger as blinking green check marks blossomed across the map. Some had tiny gray boxes on the map nearby with a two- or three-digit number inside, while other check marks were accompanied by a miniature blue boxes, also with numbers.

"This map has a green check mark for each reported sighting of Dawkins," Carson said.

"And the colored boxes?"

"Gray for rebel. Blue for Yankee."

"And the numbers inside each box?"

Carson turned away from me, mumbling, and for a moment he seemed to be talking to someone or something in the mist, although I studied the vapory haze rising from the floor and was unable to spot a listener.

"Say that again, please," I insisted. "I didn't catch that."

"Missing spooks." His eyes flashed with a darkness that blamed me for stirring unpleasant memories. "Missing soldiers. The numbers show how many went missing after Dawkins's visits."

"What do you mean by *missing*? They wandered off with Dawkins to find a bar? They became pacifists? Dawkins convinced them to haunt a more prestigious zip code?"

Try as I might to discover whatever else Carson knew about Dawkins, I couldn't get another word out of him. His lower lip grew nearly to the size of his head to make it perfectly clear that he was sulking. When Carson pouted, no one, least of all me, was going to deprive him of a good snit.

Death, as my buddy Hank said after meeting Carson, strikes some of us harder than others.

I DRIFTED TO a quiet corner of the walk-in freezer.

Once you accept that spooks can't interact with pens or keyboards, but we are able to write upon fog, smoke and other fluffy media, any doubts about Carson having access to the personnel database of both Yankee and Confederate spectral armed forces shrivel into insignificance. Let's just accept that he can and he did.

Certainly, I don't have any reason to distrust Carson. Dawkins was neither bluecoat nor rebel, and I wasn't the only spook on which he had a strange effect. The simplest explanation for Carson's map with its numbers about spectral disappearances was that no one wanted to hang around the neighborhood if they were likely to bump into the likes of Dawkins. Hadn't that been exactly what I saw when he was chased away from the spooks at Belle Island and kept from boarding the ghost ships?

For that matter, knocking over the spotlight in the theater a few nights ago could've been just another skirmish in his ongoing campaign to make the afterlife as miserable as possible for his fellow spirits.

Intriguing nuggets of speculation and data were strewn in front of me, but try as I might, I couldn't pretend any longer that I had a reason for delaying my transcendence. Whatever Dawkins's motivation, he wasn't my problem.

When I looked for *the next left thing to do* I was confronted with a vast and empty abyss. My to-do list was empty. My obligations were met. My expectations were zeroed out. Nothing stood between me and my transcendence except my own reluctance to leave the quirky, irksome, unpredictable and occasionally obnoxious spooks who have shaped my afterlife. And perhaps that's the point I should stay focused on. All of my incentives for transcending are positive ones. I can't think of a single spook I want to get away from, not even Dawkins.

"We don't take orders from her." Private Carson was talking to someone on the other side of a stack of oranges. "If I'm not mistaken, the Colonel is still in charge here."

"It's not so much *orders*," came the tentative, raspy reply. "The men would rather spend time with her."

What's this, I said to myself. An astral floozy?

"But an entire battalion?" Carson asked.

The conversation was more interesting than anything I could come up with by myself. I drifted closer.

"Not all at once," the hidden speaker said.

"That's good," Carson said.

"There's only room at the table for three or four at a time," the stranger said.

I could practically hear Carson's squinty look. "We're here to fight, not to play cards."

Wasn't someone just talking about the joys of not knowing a single spook he wanted to avoid in the afterlife? Oh, yeah, that was me.

Twenty-Six

CHAPTER

In a maneuver that required a deftly executed *poof*, followed immediately by another well-timed *poof*, I was back at the Delta Tau Chi house on Harrison Street.

Enough of Dawkins and the peculiar drummer he was following. Death isn't supposed to give anyone a headache. If Dawkins wasn't a Yankee and wasn't a rebel, was anything left? I needed to restore my sense of what was paranormal, hence, my side trip to the porch on Harrison Street strewn with beer cans and gym socks set out for fumigation.

A line of rebels stretched out the front door, across the porch, down the sidewalk and halfway into the next block, while on either side officers from the spectral cavalry urged the troops to return to their units. *(Note to readers: The spectral cavalry has all the accoutrements of the first-life cavalry, except for the horses and the junk that helps you aim them.)*

Hoots and growls followed me as I cut through the line and slipped into the house.

While I had been talking to Private Carson at the rebel intelligence center inside the freezer, Esmee had been busy. She was back at the table floating above the physical card table in the basement. No Sunshiners were in evidence except for two young men passed out on the sofas.

Esmee tapped the deck of cards in front of her, waiting for things to settle down. She was the dealer and, mercifully, the large cigar she sported earlier had found a home elsewhere. Three rebels on the opposite side of the table studied their ectoplasmic cards with one pressing his face so closely to his hand that I might've thought he read his cards with his nose. I knew the other players: Fast Eddie, Hank, Big G, Jingle Jim, Roger, and, in a surprise that would have knocked the remaining breath from of a lesser spook, my sponsor Cal.

"We'll deal you in when someone drops out," Cal told me, glancing up from his cards.

"Which ought to be now," Big G added. "Call."

The trio of rebels were nervous. I know. I could look right through them; so could every other spook in the room. They were as transparent as hummingbirds' wings. They'd been gambling with their own ectoplasm, now placed in glittery puddles in front of Esmee. You didn't have to know poker to see who was being washed by the tides of fortune and who was being taken to the cleaners.

One of the rebels was on the verge of slipping into nothingness. His spectral essence was concentrated in his hands and eyeballs.

"Pair of threes," Esmee exclaimed, slapping down her cards.

The rebs groaned. "So long, Shadrach," one said. "It's been nice seeing you."

"Let my short and pitiful time among you be a warning," Shadrach whispered. "Beware of the dangers of old cards and loose women."

"Loose women, loose women!" Esmee growled. "You're calling me a loose woman?"

The ghost of an Adam's apple hung high on Shadrach's throat. "Yes, ma'am. That you are. Now that I'm set to ride the winds for all eternity, I can't flinch from the truth."

Esmee smiled shyly. "Well, if you aren't a silver-tongued charmer. I gotta show you how much I appreciate that."

Shadrach blushed or at least a pink tint overtook his tentative being. "For Roth's sake, ma'am. I've lost everything. Must you torture me too?"

Esmee pushed the ectoplasm across the table to Shadrach and his friends. "Why don't you boys share this? There's already too much of me for one afterlife."

Hungrily, the rebels scooped up the precious liquid and squeezed it into their transparent figures, and I saw the shadows of the afterlife return to their forms, plumping them up with the vibrancy of postmortality.

While Roger escorted them from the table and brought in more gamblers to join the game, Esmee shuffled the ectoplasmic cards, Hank poked his head through the basement window to see if it was snowing; and Cal glanced in my direction.

We can't have the calm before the storm without having the storm, I thought as Cal glided toward me.

"Wasn't that a nice gesture on Esmee's part?" he said. "Why take someone else's ectoplasm?"

"She's a champ."

Cal crossed his arms over his chest. He'd already exceeded his weekly quota for chitchat and if he didn't get to the point quickly, he might lose all self-control. Who knows what would happen? He might take up the tango or dedicate his second life to developing a perpetual motion machine or figure out a way to smile.

"It's been a few nights since I've seen you at a meeting," he said. "Are you planning to come tonight after the play?"

"Wouldn't miss it for the afterworld. Anything to help a buddy break the sunshine habit."

I patted his shoulder to make sure he understood which buddy I thought was most in need of my guidance.

If words were calculated to annoy – and mine were craftily wrought to have that effect on Cal – the old spook should be recrossing his arms for the next half hour and studying the beer stains in the carpet for clues about what to say next.

Instead, he patted my shoulder, shot a look at the door and said, "That's good to hear, Ralph. Look, I gotta go talk to the newest spook I'm sponsoring."

He left me drifting in the middle of the room. Alone. Sponsorless. While he greeted a spook who was coming to him for help working the 12-step recovery program of Specters Anonymous. A spook who looked like he'd been dragged so often through the garbage during his first life that he hauled a quarter ton of muck into the afterlife.

A spook who went by the name of Dawkins.

Before you decide what you should do or say, began one of Rosetta's gems, *ask yourself what a reasonable spook would do or say.* To which I usually added, *then go in the opposite direction.*

I decided to invite myself into the conversation between Cal and Dawkins. As I was crossing the room, Cal was diverted by Jingle Jim to adjudicate a dispute with Esmee that involved placing the deck face-up in her lap to slip cards into certain locations before she dealt them.

Which left me and Dawkins without adult supervision.

"I've been around a while," I said, wasting no time, "but I never believed that I'd see Yankees and rebels united in their joint interest in getting away from a single spook."

Dawkins's features were barely visible through the layer of ash that covered his face. However, there was no mistaking the cold, steady darkness of his eyes. "If that's what you think, then you're only seeing half of what's going on."

"Meaning?"

"They're not just leaving here. They're going to someplace else."

A feather could've knocked me into the next county, assuming I could find ownerless plumage that interacts with spectral entities. I'd been willing to believe many unpleasant things about Dawkins, but not that he was a simple idiot. No other explanation was possible. Who else but an idiot would glide – on purpose – into the middle of a fight that's been going on for a century and a half?

His confidence put me in mind of a spook named Randall who once tried to run things in the hereafter. Randall didn't last long enough to get a proper title – king of the astral hill, demonic dictator, eternal president or simply Uber-Spirit were the leading contenders – but Dawkins was beginning to strike me as being cut from the same piece of spectral cloth.

"So where are they?" I asked. "Those troops who are someplace else?"

Dawkins had a grin that was colder than a dead banker's heart. "Let's just call it a better place."

"Then everything is peachy," I said, trying to slather on so much sarcasm that even a spirit as clueless as Dawkins would notice.

But he didn't. He drifted across the room and waited patiently next to Cal as Cal tried to pry the deck of cards from Esmee's cold fingers. A crisis was averted when Big G yanked the cards while Cal had her distracted and, cigar stub on full alert, shuffled the deck himself. Every spook in the room watched developments at the table with the attention usually reserved for sputtering fuses.

After Big G slid the deck back to Esmee, she shook her hands as though working out a cramp. Her smile was angelic. All that mattered to her was to be the dealer.

Cal and Dawkins drifted to a corner of the room. Cal crossed his arms and stared at Dawkins's feet, a posture familiar to me, as was Dawkins's rush to get to the point of whatever he had to say before Cal froze into that position and was unable to move. I've had that same worry on many a night.

Back at the table, Jingle Jim was mumbling through a series of nonsense syllables in search of a rhyme for chimney. Three new arrivals laid their rifles and pistols on the table and began converting those weapons into pure ectoplasm while Fast Eddie tried to convince them it'd be in everyone's interest to let him see their cards before placing any bets.

Meanwhile, Gilda had slipped into the room and made herself comfortable above a couch with a snoring frat brother. Her hands were folded in her Pollyanna-ish lap, her simple white slippers primly pressed together, her eyes as bright as the day she was buried.

I went over to Gilda. "Have you come here to gloat or to join the game?" I asked.

"I don't play games of chance. We're dead. Chance doesn't apply to us anymore. As for gloating, I have no idea what you could possibly mean."

"Then what words would you use to describe yourself?"

"Serene, content, secure in the wisdom of our 12-step program."

"Are you sure you're talking about yourself?" I said.

"I'm certainly not talking about you."

"So long as you're not gloating."

She worked to squeeze the crinkles from her lips. "I never gloat."

I resumed my place by the card table. With Esmee dealing, the ectoplasmic cards spun from her fingers like snowflakes in a blizzard. *Chance doesn't apply to us.* Then what does? Predestination? Free will? Is the afterlife a field we can cross in any direction? Is there a path? Or a chute?

Or, putting the question into an appropriate context, if death is a card game, what happens after you've played your last card?

Get another last card, an inner voice told me.

Twenty-seven

CHAPTER

So I went back to Margie's, where a half dozen Breathers were scattered across the waiting room and not a single spook was in evidence. My astral friends were either in the card game at the frat house or heading to the Byrd theater for the world's first interdimensional holiday play.

Margie's paying customers stared silently at the twinkling lights that outlined the bay window, highlighting the world's ugliest vase on the sill. Each client was wrapped in insecurities thicker than the winter coats draped over the backs of chairs and sofas, and I was struck by how dull – dare I say, lifeless – their time in the sunshine must be without us spooks.

"Hhhhsssttt. Hey, Godhead, over here." The vase in the bay window was trying to get my attention.

The *hhhhsssttt* came from Sniveler, one of the three spooks entombed in the ghastly pot. Truth be told, I didn't feel much like a deity at the moment. I sidled in the other direction, halfway across the waiting room next to a coed with a multicolored scarf looped around her neck and a cell phone growing from one hand.

In the physical world, the young woman was checking her email. In my postmortal world, Spunky emerged from the cell phone, with half his face covered by a strange white mask that stretched from his untamed, curly hair to the top of his jaw.

Spunky reached for me with one hand while clasping the silken fabric of a cape over his shoulders. He sang: "Dah, dah, DAH . . . the music of the NIGHT."

I recoiled. A spook pretending he's a fictional character who's pretending to be an actor who's pretending to be a phantom. Plausibility collided with implausibility, and chaos rippled from that cell phone in clumps that didn't know whether they were particles, waves, gases or pitchers of iced tea.

(Note to readers: This phenomenon is known as a Vonnegut Maelstrom, when fiction and non-fiction become so intertwined that it's impossible to figure out whether the socks on the floor belong to the main character, the author, the reader or Billy Pilgrim.)

"What did you tell Letitia?" a voice hissed at my elbow.

"What?"

Glancing down, I realized I had backed into the bay window, where Sniveler was whispering from the ugly purple vase.

"What were you and Letitia talking about?" Sniveler said. "Back a few nights ago, the last time you were here?"

I glanced at Spunky. With the dignity of an offended earl, he wrapped the cape across his chest and slowly funneled into the coed's cell phone.

"What did you say to her, Your Almightiness? She hasn't been the same since your talk."

My focus shifted to Sniveler and the vase and his question about Letitia, although, having come so close to being sucked down a feasibility vortex, I was too rattled to put much stock in anything that passes for an existence.

Sniveler's other companion in the vase, Whiner, intervened.

"Stop that this instant. You can't go around interrogating the Great God Ralph, like he's some run-of-the-mill divinity. It's not done."

"I was just asking a question, is all," Sniveler sniveled.

"Well, cut it out." Whiner was showing more backbone than he was probably allowed.

Me? I drifted away from the window again, giving plenty of space to the handful of Sunshiners in the waiting room with cell phones in their hands.

Without intending to, without having more than a smidgen of consciousness about what was happening, I darted through the strings of beads hanging over a doorway and shot down the corridor where Sophie's old Psychic Parlor was on the left, Margie's current Counseling Workshop was on right and, at the end, nestled in shadows, was the locked door to Margie's private apartment.

I gave that door a chilly appraisal and slipped inside.

CHAPTER

Twenty-eight

wo minutes later, I was back in the corridor. Not sure how I got there or why. Not even sure when. But there I was, with *The Honeymooners* disc behind me and Margie's voice ahead, floating down the hall from the room where she met her clients, her soft, whispered syllables making me think of slow baths on Saturday nights – me, who hasn't touched soap since my funeral – and bread baking in the oven and voices that had more important things to say than words could carry.

I could've stayed in the hallway for hours, letting the warm currents of Margie's voice wash over me, although I didn't have the slightest interest in hearing what she said because I could hear – with skull-cleansing clarity – what she meant.

Further up the hall was Esmerelda's old work space. A dust cloth sat like a prayer cap atop a crystal ball, with enough Persian rugs, brocaded thingees, tasseled whatzits and crocheted doodads to furnish a Victorian hotel. The fumes from Sophie's apricot brandy still leached from the walls.

Then to the waiting room. Half a dozen Breathers in varying stages of anxiety still hunched over their armchairs and sofas, all wrapped in their own thunderheads. Silence spewed through the room like water from ruptured hydrants. Silence and pain and confusion and self-doubt.

A momentary *poof* and I could be cheering the final stretch of tonight's tortoise derby in the Galapagos, but, as you may have sensed, I wasn't thinking clearly. I dove into the nearest refuge, which happened to be the world's ugliest purple vase on the window sill.

Suddenly, I was in a vast cavernous hall, whose walls filled the horizon like galactic bruises, and whose floor was an undulating land of purple valleys and lavender hills. Everything I saw was purple.

"If you're looking for an argument, Godie, you've come to the right flower pot." The voice was husky, overlaid with a chilliness that belied Letitia's usual honeysuckle charm.

"I need a minute to pull myself together," I said. "I'm sorry if I behaved horribly the other night."

"No," Letitia said, her voice seemed to come from all surfaces of the vase's interior at once. "You behaved rudely. I'm the one who's about to behave horribly."

"Just give me a minute."

Even though I could hear Sniveler and Whiner whispering in the distant recesses of the vase, they kept their distance. Letitia was silent, but it was the silence of a volcano whose plumes of acidic gas could be smelled miles at sea.

The vase, made by Letitia's fiance to mark the end of their engagement, was shaped from clay he mixed with Letitia's cremated remains after hastening her arrival in the afterlife. Still, the vase was officially a grave, albeit a rarity among tombs because of its tapered spout. As everyone familiar with the hereafter knows, a spook who enters another's burial site is condemned to stay there until – ah, roughly, rounding up to the nearest millennium – the end of time.

I, however, was not in the vase in the most crucial meaning of the word *in*. I was in the hollow interior of the container, whereas Letitia's cremated remains were in the ceramic shell that surrounded me. So, unlike Sniveler, Whiner or Letitia, I could leave at any time.

Not that I wanted to, despite Letitia's prickly greeting.

What I wanted was a moment to sort through the last seconds of *The Honeymooners* DVD that I saw in Margie's apartment, the very DVD I've spent my entire afterlife knowing was linked to my transcendence.

Lying microns above the bottom of the vase, not only was I unable to think about the DVD, I couldn't remember what was involved in thinking. The closest I came to a thought was: *Purple*. Purple was the color of the universe I entered in the vase. Purple. Everything was purple and that was the way it was supposed to be. That was perfectly – or *purplely* – fine with me.

Letitia's voice returned, without the angry edge. "I've never seen anyone so glum after learning their final lesson."

"That's the problem. I don't think I learned anything."

"We wouldn't be spooks if we didn't have trouble with acceptance. When I realized that for most spooks the hereafter was larger than one measly vase, I was fit to – "

"I wish acceptance was the issue for me," I mumbled.

"So, what did you see in there?"

"Nothing."

"Oh?" A hint of Letitia's old playfulness was back. "You were watching the DVD. Some character was saying something or doing something. Then the screen went blank."

"That's not it. The story had a proper ending. It's just that nothing happened. Nothing was said or done that meant anything to me."

"Hmm. Might that be your lesson?"

"I don't understand."

The scent of magnolia blossoms grew stronger; I sensed Letitia sashaying through the ceramics a few atoms from my ectoplasm. I could almost see a spectral finger waving at me beneath the ceramic skin. "Turn off your thinker. It hasn't done you much good so far."

"You think that's what I should do?"

"Think it over," Letitia purred.

THE MORE I pressed Letitia for details, the more playful and evasive she became. She was the spirit of an old-school Southern belle and couldn't resist the chance to flirt with a spook of the opposing gender. Still, I picked up a tip that could put me back on the path to transcendence: Turn off the ol' thinker and start paying attention to the afterlife around me.

By the time I was ready to leave the vase, Letitia had gone back to calling me *Godie*, Sniveler and Whiner had crept out of the purple shadows and were timidly asking if I had any preferences about graven images in my own likeness, and I realized I'd missed another nightly meeting of Specters Anonymous and was probably late for the premiere of *A Christmas Carol* in its updated, spook-sensitive version.

Faster than a gnat facing a cold supper, I exited the vase and used the trusty *Beam-Me-Up-Scotty* technique to travel the few blocks to the roof of the Byrd theater.

As Breathers streamed into the front doors under the marquee, spooks floated across the dark sky, heading to the theater singly, in groups and, in one case, in a crowd of about fifty led by Six-Step Steve, who runs an abbreviated recovery group popular in the suburbs.

(Note to readers: Although I disagree with Steve on nearly everything involving recovery, I'll give him proper credit. He says he has an abbreviated recovery program. And abbreviated recovery is exactly what he delivers.)

The Colonel was the only other spook on the theater roof, and soon he drifted toward me.

"Good evening to you, lad," he said, giving me a nod appropriate for a civilian nuisance. "The curtain hasn't lifted yet, and already your theatrical production seems quite the success. I'm grateful you've given our brethren – "

" – and sistren – "

" – a safe place to gather tonight."

"Do you still think something might happen?" I asked.

The Colonel was surveilling the neighborhood. The flow of spooks to the theater was decreasing. Tiny buds of brightness were imprinted on the night air as snow sifted through the darkness.

"I have never subscribed to the notion that I can read the mind of the enemy commander," he said. "However, if our positions were reversed, I would have been deploying troops throughout the area for the last several nights."

The strange patrols that never seemed to find each other suddenly made sense. They weren't looking for a fight but trying to avoid the enemy while moving secretly into position.

"I know we're in good hands." I gave him a thumbs-up and slipped over the side of the theater. Although spooks were gliding without incident through the roof and sides of the building, my experience with Letitia and the world's ugliest vase was too fresh. I went in through the front door below.

Paying customers scurried across the lobby to their seats, among them James William, his mother and father. Without having the beagle Petey along who understood me, I realized how great was my distance to the Breathers who shared my duplex. Spooks still packed the candy counter, ogling the gummy bears, malted milk balls, popcorn and other sweets not on the menu at our favorite diners and delis.

Roger argued with a newbie about whether gummy bears were, in fact, made out of bear meat. "You're trying to squeeze too much meaning out of a label," Roger said.

"Why else would they be called gummy *bears?*" the newbie insisted.

Maybe I shouldn't admit it, but I thought they both had a point. And speaking of points . . .

Back out the lobby, up the side of the building and to the roof I went. The Colonel hadn't moved. No other spook could look as busy as the Colonel without twitching so much as an eyelid.

"You know more about Dawkins than you've told me," I said, bluffing.

"Is that a question, a statement or" – the Colonel swung his face toward me, and my knees nearly sagged from the weariness in his eyes – "an accusation?"

"It's a dilemma," I answered, trusting my mouth to come up with something useful while my mind was still working on the diplomatic vocabulary. "You've always been honest with me, painfully honest. But why keep information to yourself when you knew I was trying to find out about Dawkins?"

"The more you know, the more you'll be inclined to press on when a prudent spook would back off."

"Dawkins isn't a Yankee and he isn't a rebel," I said, showing that I wasn't going to let mere prudence stand in my way. "What's left? And why's it important?"

Was there a third side in this ageless civil war and if so, what makes it a threat to anyone? Only one threat that I'd discovered was of any significance. "It's that you've been losing troops every time he visits the line."

The Colonel swung his tired eyes off me to study the buildings and streets and acres of shadows that surrounded the theater like a hostile sea.

Dawkins's visits to the troops and spectral ships cruising the James had always been short. He wasn't trying to change minds or to threaten. There hadn't been enough time. But what could he possibly say that would convince soldiers and sailors to desert their posts after a hundred and fifty years of faithful service?

"Has he been only talking to spooks in uniform?" I asked.

"Mostly, but not exclusively."

"Why?"

"Because my boys are more vulnerable than civilians to the hokum he's selling."

"What would that be?" I asked.

"You're not prepared to know." The lips behind the Colonel's trimmed moustache and beard tested the start of several sentences. "I don't mean to be harsh, son. I wasn't prepared for it either."

Twenty-nine

CHAPTER

t all began, as nearly as the Colonel could find the starting point, with an anonymous spook who'd taken to spending his days inside a hollow plaster bust of Carl Jung in the psychology department at the university. The spook's name, background, first-life affiliations, posthumous experiences and other relevant facts have been obscured by time and the efforts of partisans on both sides of the issue to cover whatever tracks were left on the spiritual plane, lest inquiring minds acquire ample information to reconstruct the spook's message.

"And what was the message?" I asked. "How does it tie in with a spook inside a bust in a psychology department? And why's it such a big secret if Dawkins already knows it?"

"I'll come to that sooner if you quit suggesting detours."

From the roof of the theater, snowflakes sparkled in the night. The traffic on Cary Street below seemed to die down as music began in the theater below. The play had started. Was it a trick of the shadows that made the Colonel's uniform look cleaner, his chin more determined as he went on with his tale?

The spook in the psychology department — whom we'll call Spook X for purposes of identification — acquired, over the course of years and thousands of conversations overheard between instructors and students, sufficient information about the mental processes of Breathers to develop unique insight into the workings of the postmortal mind.

Legend has it that Spook X had a vast armamentarium of theories and psychological tests that gave him more knowledge about postmortal behavior than any spook has ever achieved, not counting, of course, the unknown authors of *The Teeny Book*, which is the basic recovery guide for Specters Anonymous.

During an era when spectral fraternities were the places that the newly deceased gathered for help coping with their second lives, Spook X's legacy was destroyed. Members of an astral frat house went on a scavenger hunt one night that took them to the psychology department while Spook X was testing the spirits in a to-remain-nameless urban center of the country for signs of mental activity. Even in the afterlife, hazing can get out of control, and those frat spooks cleaned the interior of Jung's plaster bust more thoroughly than a snowplow going through an ice cream parlor.

"All that was left after years of work by poor Spook X was The Message," the Colonel said sadly. "That's what it's been called. The Message."

"And it says – "

"I'm getting to that, bye and bye."

The Message was based upon Spook X's study of hundreds of cases of transcendence over decades. He distilled what he had learned into fewer than a dozen words, and when he shared it for the first time with his faithful research assistant, the assistant disappeared. *Poof.* The assistant had transcended out of there.

"I'd call that strong confirmation of Spook X's work," the Colonel said. "But there was an unforeseen downside."

"I knew that was coming," I sighed. "Don't you just hate those unforeseen downsides?"

"Every time Spook X shared his research with another spook, they'd immediately depart to another afterworld."

"And the problem is – "

The Colonel slid his astral sword a few inches from its scabbard, then let it drop back with a heavy click. "Were the spooks really transcending, going to a better place? For all we know there may be worse planes of existence than our present environs. And what exactly in the message accounted for this transformation? Perhaps it unlocks doors that we can't begin to imagine."

"I know one way to find out," I said.

"Pardon?"

"Gotta scoot, Colonel. There's a big transcendence waiting out there with my name on it."

WHEN I ZIPPED back into the theater, the Ghost of Christmas Past was showing Ebeneezer Scrooge images from his own dreary childhood. At least, that was happening on the physical plane. On the astral dimension, things were more interesting.

For starters, to fit every spook who wanted to attend into the space between the seats and ceiling, Fast Eddie and his ushers had to be creative. They arranged the spooks so that those whose ectoplasm had eroded away the most were closer to the stage, allowing viewers in back to watch the show through them.

And what a show it was. Marley's ghost, whom Hank had cast with the ghost of Bob Marley, was bounding across the stage singing reggae classics while the Ghost of Christmas Past trod the boards in the physical play and, for the astral audience, Veronica made her grand appearance.

Marley sang, shook his dreadlocks and shimmied, while Veronica, her long brown hair hanging to her shoulders like a shroud, drifted over the footlights, every micron of her spectral form radiating the sort of disdain that only comes from the most spiritually advanced. Esmee, appearing as Ebeneezer's boyhood flame, mugged for the audience and chased Marley, having clearly fortified herself with embalming fluid at the frat house.

The Breathers, unaware of the shenanigans on the spiritual plane, were sighing as they watched young Scrooge pass the holidays alone in his boarding school, while the spooks, unconcerned with the drama on the physical plane, hooted and jeered as Esmee frolicked, Marley jiggled and Veronica's nose reached ever-higher angles. Hank, who was supposedly directing this mess, wrung his hands in the wings.

I saw Dawkins speak to Gilda and Rosetta at an edge of the spectral audience. I darted there before he could escape and told him, "We need to talk."

Dawkins barely glanced at me. "No."

"I know that you know The Message," I whispered.

"I have no idea what you're talking about."

The spooks around us were muttering and hissing now. One old fellow shoved my shoulder to keep me from blocking his view. With a flick of his head, Dawkins gestured for me to join him by the wall.

In a dark flash, Gilda appeared and changed from Pollyanna into an irritated, short-tempered, marginally controlled Goth who knew exactly where I spent my days and wasn't afraid to have a conversation at my least convenient moment. She locked her fingers on the collar of my spectral shirt and, before I could follow Dawkins, jerked me through the ceiling and onto the roof.

"Is there anything," she said, "anything at all, that you can't make worse?"

Her hands were outstretched in a way that made me wonder whether she was beseeching the Uber-Spirit for guidance or planning to crush my head.

Still, the question was intriguing. I gazed across the rooftops of Carytown as cookie-sized snowflakes twirled gently in the breeze and the reflected lights from shop windows left puddles of brightness in the upper limbs of some pines.

"I've never been accused of making the weather worse," I said.

"Only because you never tried."

"You have a point."

Gilda paced to the edge of the roof, shaking her head, her fists bouncing nervously against her hip. She turned, looked at me with a dark glimmer in her eyes, shook her head and turned away again. In the next instant, she was so close to my face that I was almost wearing her purple lipstick.

"How could you possibly think that Dawkins was a threat to anyone?" she hissed. "That spook couldn't find his way out of his own casket."

"Is that supposed to mean something to me?"

"I thought you were the ultimate free spirit." Her snow-white cheeks took on a pink tint. "You think you're free to choose what's important to your afterlife."

I was becoming sorry I'd left my coffeepot this evening. "I'm just an ordinary spook who's trying to transcend."

"Then you should have paid more attention to your *Honeymooners* DVD."

"I did, but nothing happened there."

"Exactly," she said with a triumphant flourish. The dark radiance in her eyes grew so fierce I knew she was paying a heavy price in ectoplasm.

Spooks don't stoop very well. Maybe because it's just easier to lower ourselves through the floor. But on this occasion, I was prepared to stoop by admitting I didn't have the slightest idea what she was talking about. I even asked, "What do you mean?" in a whisper that was so soft I barely heard it myself.

At that moment, the spooks who'd been in the audience of the theater below began arriving at the rooftop.

"Fifteen-minute intermission," Fast Eddie said, scooting through the rapidly growing spectral crowd. "Fifteen minutes."

A gaggle of newbies appeared between Gilda and me, intent on analyzing the symbolism of having Marley on stage throughout the first half of the play, whereas in the physical version, the Marley character has his few minutes of strutting and fretting before retiring to his dressing room for the remainder of the show.

Gilda disappeared in the jostling, jabbering crowd of spectral theatergoers. Why'd she go Pollyanna on me in the first place? She'd never been the sort of spook who'd enjoy wearing crinoline and frou-frou outfits.

Drifting up to find her in the growing spectral crowd, I saw the Colonel standing on the ledge of the rooftop overlooking the dark alley. At least I had answers for one spook.

"Dawkins was watching the play inside," I told him. "He should be here in a minute."

"Too late," the Colonel said.

Following his gaze northward, I looked over the grand homes and brick apartment houses on Mulberry and Ellwood to the roof of the hospital three blocks away lined with figures that I knew by their frozen silhouettes were watching us. They were too far away to make out much detail, although they wore wide-brimmed hats and coats that hung halfway to their knees.

Coats so similar, in fact, that they might be described as uniform, all dyed the same shade — the distance and the shadows and the light flurries made it difficult to see clearly — of brown or dark gray. Perhaps even blue.

The colonel rose twenty or thirty feet above the roof and turned slowly in the other direction. I stayed beside him until we faced the center of Carytown, the hospital at our backs. The James rolled darkly in the distance while, closer, the shops and restaurants along Cary Street had dimmed their lights and locked their doors for the night. Still, from the bookstore across the street and a pizza shack at the end of the block, strings of Christmas lights shone from the front windows.

Stretching out his arm in a better imitation of the true Ghost of Christmas Past than Marley had managed, the Colonel pointed to an alley between a used CD store and a furniture repair business where an astral spear pointed at us.

No, not a spear, for I recognized the small flag fixed to the end. The colors of the 27th Alabama Infantry (Spectral). A gust of wind swept away the flurries as though a curtain had been pulled aside, and I saw the motley gray uniforms of dozens of rebel fighters, stacked up four or five spooks high in the mouth of the alley.

Bayonets fashioned from ectoplasm slashed the night, astral rifles pumped with energy. Faces specterized in the murk, all with clenched teeth that could be grins or grimaces.

"That ought to persuade the Yankees to go somewhere else for their fun," I told the Colonel.

"The Yankees, it appears, have their own plans."

"What kind of a ruckus can a half dozen spooks on a roof stir up?"

The Colonel waved a hand over his shoulder, indicating the area near the hospital. "Them and ten or fifteen thousand of their friends working their way in the shadows in our direction."

I glanced behind me, then across Cary Street, where rebel outfits were marching from the side streets and gliding around houses and businesses in a silent gray wave.

"That puts us smack in the middle," I said.

"*Smack* is a good description." A slight smile flickered across the Colonel's solemn features. "Understated, but clear."

I didn't need to be a tactician to know what would happen next. Ectoplasmic bullets and astral bayonets can't do lasting damage to a spook, but, as one who's found himself at the wrong end of an armed ghost more than once, I can testify that it's not an experience that anyone enjoys.

More damaging would be the effect of a firefight on the wide-eyed newbies watching the play who had been spending their hereafters hiding in the shadows alone and rarely venturing out. We won't see them again if this rooftop becomes a battlefield. They'd burrow into a granite mountain out west and stay there until their ectoplasm wears away from sheer gravity. They'll never transcend to a higher dimension or even know that they can.

CHAPTER Thirty

ilda and Hank joined us fifty feet above the festive intermission on the rooftop where spooks were unaware of both the Union forces concentrating north of the theater, becoming a dark blotch on the snowy streets and tiny lawns, and the rebels massing in the alleys and side streets on the other side of the building.

I could've believed Hank was watching a tennis match from the way his head swung from one shoulder to the other to observe the maneuvering forces. "From this angle," he said, "a lot of that military stuff about strategy and tactics makes sense."

"Lucky you. You get to spend some quality time in the middle of a battlefield," Gilda sniped. Her black leather gleamed and her chains jangled confidently. She was back in full Goth array.

"What did you mean earlier about Dawkins?" I asked. "You seem pretty sure you know what he's capable of doing."

Like a rocky shoreline coming into view seconds after the captain realizes his ship is off course, a vague notion began to take shape in my mind.

"Was your Pollyanna getup a way of getting closer to Dawkins?" I asked.

"No, but as Generalissimo Hank would say, it was useful camouflage."

"And Dawkins told you things he wouldn't have said if you were—" I took stock of my situation, my highly delicate, easily explosive situation "—properly dressed, as you are now."

"Could be," she said. "Could be."

"So you know The Message," I said, regretting every snarky thing I'd ever told her. "Tell me."

"No." The look Gilda gave me should be pasted into every dictionary next to the phrase *steely-eyed*.

I'm not too proud to beg. I'm not even above groveling. But I was desperate, not stupid, and I knew that Gilda wouldn't be influenced by my pleas to find out The Message. Whether I wanted to or not, I had to recognize that fixing this mess was my *next left thing*.

From the corner of my eye, I saw Dawkins hover over a corner of the roof where he could watch both rebels and Yankees assemble on the streets for the coming battle. I also saw Cal and Rosetta on the edge of the crowd, watching me. I glided toward them.

"I was just wondering what Cal would do in a situation like this," I said, taking in both armies with a grand sweep of my arm. "Maybe the master could enlighten me."

Yeah, set my ectoplasm on fire, and I'll still do *glib* better than anyone else in Happily-Ever-After.

Cal crossed his arms over his chest with an air of deliberation. "Funny you should mention that. You aren't the only one wondering what I should do."

I grinned at him. He tightened his grip on his own arms. I grinned at Rosetta. She seemed lost in memories of biting into a lemon.

The Colonel left to rejoin his troops with a courtly salute. I checked Dawkins, now no longer alone in his corner overlooking the two armies. The Somber Sisters were also there: three ashen figures facing him in a silent row, each colored the same sort of vague gray that Dawkins had.

Whatever the Somber Sisters didn't say, they must've didn't say it very convincingly, for Dawkins's hulking, stormy figure began to change. The suggestion of a head wearing a military-style cap dissolved into a lump in the middle of shoulders that became a wider lump atop a lead-colored confabulation of mists that was soon indistinguishable from the three original Somber Sisters.

Now four Sisters strong, they glided from the ledge to the center of the partying spooks. Somber as always, they gave everyone the uncomfortable feeling that he / she / it was being scrutinized and, so far, everyone had been found wanting.

"Thank the Uber-Spirit that it's over," Rosetta whispered to Cal. "I'm surprised it lasted this long."

"These things last as long as they last," Cal replied.

Personally, I didn't die to keep running into surprises. Put that together with Zen-like sayings from Cal and Veronica, and my ability to suppress my inner snark was seriously weakened.

"You knew Dawkins was one of the Somber Sisters," I said.

"Yep," Cal said.

"Didn't everyone," Rosetta added.

"But . . . I mean . . . when you . . ."

Cal shuffled to get a better view of the streets below. "The Somber Sisters have always believed in setting a proper example for the newly deceased. Sure, they disagree with Specters Anonymous and those of us who have meetings and talk about our problems transcending. But they've always expressed their disagreement by their silent, dignified presence, not by anything they said or did."

"Dawkins broke the mold," I said.

"He thought he found something everyone needed to know." Rosetta was the soul of reasonableness, except for those who mangled the language or don't know how to properly set a table. "He felt an obligation to share what he'd learned with the rest of us."

"The Message," I said.

Cal scuffed a toe through the asphalt roof. "I'll give him credit. The Message helped a lot of spooks who were still in uniform. Unfortunately, commanders on both sides thought it was a ploy by their enemies to weaken their forces."

"Which explains how we got into tonight's face-off," I summed up. "Has there ever been a bigger jerk on this side of the Great Divide than Dawkins?"

"No, no, no," Gilda said, rising from the sidelines. "You have to give Dawkins credit. He saw this coming. That's why he tried to sabotage the play."

I could no longer see the units creeping toward the theater, but my spectral senses felt them moving through the snow-clouded night, rifles at the ready, anger in whatever passes for their hearts.

"Does The Message say anything that could create a little peace now?" I asked.

"Indisputably," Rosetta sniffed. "However, I believe all parties have already heard The Message. By their armed presence here tonight, they're showing it has no effect upon them."

ka-FFT.

A shot from an ectoplasmic rifle split the darkness. The spooks on the theater roof broke into cheers and applause. They thought fireworks were part of the show.

ka-FFT, ka-FFT, ka-FFT. A ragged volley sputtered below on the streets from several sides of the building. Spooks rushed to the edges of the roof for a better view of the entertainment.

"I'm open to suggestions," Cal said.

"A white flag?" Gilda suggested.

"A counterattack." Hank's fists were encased in ectoplasmic chain mail.

Veronica crept up on us like a bad smell. She was dressed in her usual simple brown smock; her long brunette hair hung straight to her shoulders as though each follicle had been bullied into place.

Cal and Rosetta traded a look. They weren't going to solve any problems for us, including the problem most of us had with the way Veronica treated everyone as though we weren't the sort of posthumous friends that folks were dying to meet.

"If you want peace," Veronica intoned, "then you must *be* the peace."

She gazed down her nose at us, and I fought the urge to respecterize some ectoplasm into an oversized ant's antenna to wriggle back at her.

"Rubbish," Gilda murmured, then, catching Veronica's eye, added: "Sorry. I meant that we must *be* the rubbish."

Gilda would give Veronica a fair fight in any outbreak of verbal fisticuffs, but Veronica didn't seem inclined at the moment to do anything fairly. She offered me the benefit of her attention.

"I don't suppose you know what peace is," she told me. "The Mahareshrash says that peace is the paranormal state of — "

I let her babble on. Despite ghostly rifles coughing out their ectoplasmic bullets, the hubbub continued on the rooftop over the wonderful display of fireworks in the streets. Nothing quite as grand as the New Caledonia Precision Spectral Flying team, of course, but what is? I watched snowflakes streaming across the night sky.

Each flake a benediction, an upbeat little ditty, a spark of hope floating toward the benighted earth. And I remembered my own escape a few nights ago when I hid my shrunken self in a passing flurry and submitted my destiny to the whims of a midwinter breeze.

Surely, that was peace.

I snapped out of my reverie to find Veronica studying me down a nose that was long enough to land a Boeing 747.

"Have you heard the slightest thing I said?" Veronica asked me.

"The slightest thing?" I replied in innocence. "I don't care how many spooks say you're slight. I think you have an interesting point."

Cal says a responsible spook checks with his sponsor before making a major decision. I tell Cal I'll keep that in mind the moment I become responsible. Back to treetop height I zoomed, centered myself squarely above the middle of the rooftop and clapped my astral hands for attention.

"Spooks, specters and spectacles. We're going to have audience participation during the second half of our play," I announced. "Before intermission ends and we go down for the rest of the performance, perhaps we should rehearse our part."

Titters and chuckles greeted my little speech, with the occasional guffaw and at least one clear harrumph.

"What's our part?" a spook on the rooftop shouted.

"Snowflakes. We're going to be the snowstorm that appears at the end of the play."

My friend Jedidiah later said the spectral laughter that followed my announcement was loud enough to reach him in the cemetery. "It was just like thunder," he told me. "Except it was the exact opposite."

CHAPTER
Thirty-one

nowflakes smaller than mosquitoes, snowflakes larger than an elephant's ear, each crystalline figure unique in all of specterdom, we circled above the theater with the dignity of royal yachts cruising the Nile.

Once all the spooks on the rooftop had assumed distinctive snowflake shapes, we whirled and looped above Carytown, growing thick enough to hide tree trunks from the flakes pirouetting at the end of the boughs, and when I was sure the last of the spectral stragglers had caught up with us, I led the shimmering squall to street level.

We caromed around the block as a maelstrom of white, a snowy wind, a speckled ivory curtain that swirled between the approaching armies, then between individual soldiers, and finally becoming thick enough to hide ectoplasmic rifles from the spooks who were carrying them, muffling orders, whiting out flags, wrapping each soldier in a frosty cocoon that seemed so tenacious that most respecterized their weapons – and themselves – into downy snowflakes to join the blizzard.

At some point I became aware of a blotch moving through the flurry, and when I spiraled over to investigate, ended inches from a cold, disapproving presence. Or, rather, four presences. The Somber Sisters were making their way through the snow and snow-like spooks, bound for their hideaway in the collapsed tunnel where they would spend a century or two shielded from anyone who chose to look on the bright side of the tombstone.

One of the four hesitated and turned in my direction, and I'd like to think it was Dawkins, wishing me better luck spreading the message of Specters Anonymous than he had with his cryptic lesson.

BY THE TIME we made it back into the theater, the respiring audience was gone, and the only ones remaining were two janitors picking litter under the seats and Marley's ghost, still shaking his dreadlocks to a reggae beat.

One-by-one, then by the dozens and finally by the hundreds, snowflakes changed back into spooks. A few settled above the empty seats to enjoy Marley's performance, most left through the walls and ceiling of the theater to resume their nightly routines, but every spectral face nearly glowed with excitement.

Some snowflakes transformed themselves into spooks wearing Union blue and grins that took on a rictus of alarm when they saw the crowd in which they were mingling. They left so quickly their *poofs* sounded unsure about what had just happened. Meanwhile, spooks in gray flocked to the balcony, having had enough marching, counter-marching, double-timing and route-stepping for one night.

Spunky emerged from the cell phone clipped to a janitor's belt. The brim of a dark fedora slouched over his eyes; the upturned collar of a trench coat hid his chin.

"Of all the sepulchers, in all the cemeteries, in all of the afterlife, she gets planted in mine," he lisped, finishing with a twitch under an eye and a weird ripple along his upper lip.

"I'm sorry this didn't work out for you, Spunky," I said.

"Didn't work out? You gotta be kidding."

"I don't understand."

"At the end of the play, when the Breathers on stage came back for their final bows, everyone sang *I'm Dreaming of a White Christmas*. I'm talking about the cast, the spooks, the audience, the ushers, even the kids running the candy counter. Every Spunky in the joint popped out of his cell phone and digital watch to sing along. I even saw a few Spunkies take time from overseeing their pacemakers to join the chorus."

"I'm sorry I missed that."

Spunky winked at me. "You're going to have a tough time topping this next year. But I know you're just the spook who can do the job."

"It helps to have a plan," I said, adding after he despecterized back into his cell phone, "Or maybe not."

I LET MYSELF get swept up in the spooks leaving the theater after Marley finished his reggae favorites and went into his own impressions of Humphrey Bogart. Been there, done that, seen the headstone.

Eventually, the regulars from the St. Sears meeting ended up at our favorite diner in Shockoe Bottom, where the desserts were generous and the patrons never complained about the drafts that were actually Fast Eddie or Mrs. Hannity or another member of the spectral gang trying to pry loose a few tasty molecules of apple pie *a la mode*.

I headed for a booth in the back of the upper level and ended up alongside a middle-aged couple who seemed anxious to get back on the road. He had an omelet, she a soup and salad and they took turns looking at their wristwatches. For once, I didn't try to hone my skills as a people-whisperer by planting the suggestion that a nice chocolate milk shake would really hit the spot about now.

"A penny for your thoughts," Gilda said, gliding down beside me. She was her paranormal self, with black leather, chains and purple cosmetics.

"You haven't got a penny," I answered.

"And you don't have a thought." She smiled sweetly. "But I wanted to ask anyway."

Ain't it nice when friends gather around for the holidays?

I jabbed a finger in the vicinity of her purple fingernails. "So, your time as Pollyanna wasn't a trick to find out what Dawkins was up to."

"Not entirely. I really wanted to see what it was like to glide a few miles in Pollyanna's ectoplasm."

"What was it like?"

She shuddered. "If I wanted to be an optimist, I'd've kept breathing. Anyhow, it helped me understand Dawkins once he showed up. He seemed more relaxed around Pollyanna than a Goth."

"Yeah, some spooks can't tolerate an assertive woman."

"I know," she said, giving me that look. And I mean, *that* look.

I tried giving it back, but she wasn't taking anything from me. "So, what was Dawkins telling everyone? What's The Message?"

Unease flickered across Gilda's features. "I don't think I'm qualified to decide whether you can handle that. Where's Cal?"

She scanned the tables and booths for my sponsor, spotted him by a stool near the front door and waved him over. Tough as it was, as out-of-character as it was, I had to repress my natural snarkiness. I had seconds to ask an unsupervised question or two while Gilda's fortress-like defenses were temporarily offline. Before I could get my mouth in motion, she asked:

"Did you really see the end of Margie's *Honeymooners* DVD?"

"I did."

"And nothing there made you want to transcend?"

I gave her a what-the-Roth twitch of my hands. "I'm still here."

Cal, gentlespook that he was, waited as the Breather couple scooped up the last soggy remnants of their dessert and slid from the booth, taking their coats and the bill to the cash register. Cal settled next to Gilda. No one had to remind him to keep an eye on me.

"Ralph says he's seen all of Margie's *Honeymooner's* DVDs," Gilda said. "Nothing did anything for him."

"Not even a little?" Cal sounded too hopeful.

"Any chance there might be a delayed effect?" I asked.

Cal ran his astral fingers over the top of the table. "The point of transcendence is that we finally learn a lesson that we missed on the physical plane. Are you sure there wasn't something important there?"

I pondered his question for a couple of seconds, which was about 1.98 seconds longer than I needed.

"Nothing jumped out at me, Cal. Ralph Kramden had a problem, he and his friends tried to fix it. At first they got everything wrong. They bumbled around for a while, then they got it right. In the end, they sat at the kitchen table, smiling and cozy, and everything was wonderful. And I was smiling along with them and thinking that they'll be okay now that they've straightened out that problem. But nothing stays fixed forever. Something else has gotta go wrong soon."

"Sounds like a life," Cal said. "Or an afterlife."

Cal gazed over my shoulder at the front of the diner where an automated Santa Claus doll stood in the window waving at the quiet, empty streets. The snowfall had dwindled to a sputter, and somewhere in the darkness a dog was looking for a warm place to poop.

My sponsor's thoughtful mood made me uncomfortable. Shouldn't a part of him be happy that I wasn't leaving his afterlife? Or was he upset that his personal Ghost of Christmas Future had my face?

Gilda was obviously fighting off her own case of the Why-Is-Ralph-Still-Here blues. She turned to Cal. "Ralph's wondering about Dawkins's message. Do you think we should tell him?"

"What harm can it do?" Cal said, although I was getting better at reading his mind and knew he really wanted to say, *Sure, maybe he'll even poof out of here for good.*

"Are you ready?" Gilda stared at me, hard, and I could've sworn one of the chains over her shoulder reared up for a moment like a cobra testing the air for prey.

I gripped the table. My fingers met each other in the middle of the wood. I got a firmer grip on myself.

"Go," I said.

"Here it is: All grudges come with an expiration date."

I waited for her to finish. Then I waited some more.

Moments like this are tough in the hereafter. There's no dramatic emphasis in continuing to hold my breath. I can't break out in a sweat, although I could squeeze droplets of ectoplasm to my astral forehead, but how would that help me or anyone else?

"Not doing anything, huh?" Gilda said.

"Nope."

Again there was a breathless moment that might have been fraught with significance if all my moments since the funeral hadn't been breathless.

"What do we do now?" I asked.

Gilda looked at Cal. Cal looked at me. And in a chorus the three of us said:

"Let's go to a meeting."

And we drifted into the night, pilgrims on an unending search for the wisdom and understanding of a 12-step meeting, as a chorus of voices rose behind us in the diner, singing *Spunky, the Frosted Wraith*.

— The End —

A preview follows

Of the eighth novel in the Specters Anonymous series

THE GHOST WITH THE GLASS EYE

Available Halloween 2020 on Kindle and Amazon.Com

Also available are the first seven books in the series:

Specters Anonymous (Book 1)

Nelle, Nook and Randall (Book 2)

The Infernal Task of Aemon T. Lado (Book 3)

Died and Gone to Richmond (Book 4)

Heck's Angels (Book 5)

Spook Noir (Book 6)

A Christmas Wraith (Book 7)

THE GHOST WITH THE GLASS EYE

CHAPTER ONE

Nothing typified the Ghost with the Glass Eye so much as his arrival. Like everything about him, the question at hand always seemed to be in someone else's pocket and instead of focusing on the important issues – such as, who was this new guy, where did he come from, and what was he doing in our neighborhood – each discussion had a way of slaloming into an argument about who saw him first.

Me? I avoided the debate because I knew with absolute certainty that I had spotted GeeGee long before anyone else. It was on the night our meeting room turned into a junkyard. Not the sort of detail one forgets.

I had arrived in the church basement to find dozens of folding cots lazing on their sides against the walls as though too pooped to stand on their own four legs. Cardboard boxes in different stages of assembly or decomposition ranged across the floor, some with old sheets hanging down their sides like exhausted tongues, while others were topped by shaky pyramids of towels, water bottles and toys.

"A fitting place for your get-together," my old pal Gned said as we surveyed the chaos.

"'Natch. Nothing like a battlefield to make my friends feel at home." Being irked by the mess, I couldn't help from giving my words a double helping of irony.

Usually, I don't worry about impressing folks – in fact, you might say I've outlived that inclination – but this was the first visit here for Gned and he deserved the chance to form a positive opinion about the meeting.

With the slightest dip of his tall hat, he indicated the ceiling in the corner where a jumble of wires poked through the overhead tiles, creating in the dim light and shadows a passable replica of a nest of snakes who'd dropped down for a visit.

"I see you invited the vipers," Gned said with fake innocence.

"They let me in, didn't they?" I replied. "Besides, I think those are cobras."

Gned's not a very demonstrative guy. For him, the hint of a smile that played across his face was the equivalent of me putting on a wide, red-lipped, Bozo-the-Clown grin.

Even so, Gned's smile didn't last long. A commanding voice behind us barked: "This will not do. This simply will not do."

Rosetta, the leader of our support group, swept around us in a state of acute vexation. A few more wires slid back into the ceiling rather than tangle with her.

"We've been in worse places," I said.

"Quite true," Rosetta sniffed. "But this is *our* place. We're responsible here."

Gned almost blinked as he whispered, "Is she always like this?"

"Only on a good night. Let's get out of here before she thinks of something for us to do."

And that, surprisingly enough, was my last practical advice for the evening.

GNED, YOU SEE, is a gnome, a proud member of a family of the lawn ornaments. His job description is limited to guarding a quarter acre of grass.

Sporting baggy yellow trousers, a rumpled blue jacket that probably hid dozens of pockets and a pointy red hat, Gned spent most of his time on the edge of the garden, just a leaf or two into the zinnias.

I've never known him to stretch his legs or twitch an eyebrow. For that matter, the twinkle in his eyes that I saw earlier and that hint of a smile could have been a trick of the shadows. As for getting around, I can't explain what he does; I just accept that he does it.

On this particular evening, Gned the Gnome was fascinated by Rosetta as she stalked toward a packing crate in the middle of the dark, cluttered room. Guess they don't have many confrontations in the rose patch. Since I only showed up tonight for Gned's sake, I decided to leave before my reputation for inappropriate remarks got both of us in trouble. Quietly exiting through the door, I found Gned already perched on a metal rail at the top of the stairs.

"With Rosetta already there, I figure you don't need me to introduce you to the group," I said.

"I can come back tomorrow."

I studied the door at the bottom of the stairs, calculating how much I wanted Gned to know about my personal problems, but I needn't've bothered.

Before I looked up, the gnome had edged closer to me on the railing, his squat little body angled to study me from a corner of his eyes.

"So, the word getting around the cemetery is true," he said. "You're not too keen on your group meetings anymore."

"I wouldn't call it *not too keen*," I replied.

I blinked, and Gned had gotten closer.

"What would you call it?" he asked.

Crisis of confidence were the first words to pop into my mind. My commitment to my favorite support group had taken a beating lately, although enough respect remained that I wouldn't discourage Gned from giving it a try.

Time to change the subject. "Why'd you suddenly get interested in a 12-step program? Why now?"

"If it's right in front of you, it's worth studying," he said, repeating one of the basic tenets of the gnome's creed. As usually happens, I couldn't see his mouth move.

"— And if it's worth studying," added a figure slinking across the lawn toward us, "it's worth investigating very, very closely."

Gilda arrived with a trench coat, a fedora tipped rakishly over one eye and a squint, all standard issue for the staff of the Triple A detective agency.

"Nobody touches a thing, see?" she lisped. "We gotta dust for fingerprints."

Mrs. Hannity pulled up beside her. "I can't tell you how relieved I am to hear you say that, dearie. That room has needed a good dusting for ages. Maybe we could do the windows too."

Gilda's upper lip curled. Was she really going to challenge Mrs. Hannity, the group's official grandmother, with her wire-rimmed spectacles perched on the end of her nose and a cute little sag to the corners of her mouth that made her look as though she was worried someone would stick a finger into a light socket?

Then the newbies arrived, in twos and threes, bringing more mayhem as they swept Gilda and Mrs. Hannity through the basement door with the crowd. I was shoved inside too. Gned, of course, was already there.

The newbies lined up against the walls like fatalists killing time until the firing squad arrived. Soon Cal, Veronica, Fast Eddie, Esmerelda, Toni, Jingle Jim and most of the regulars trickled in, all with their own ideas for how the group should deal with, fix, avoid or protest the wires hanging from the ceiling and the cardboard boxes strewn across the floor.

My favorite tangent came from Roger, who made the case that, as a 12-step meeting, we couldn't properly eject the boxes or wires from the room until we ascertained whether they were seeking our help to recover from some unique addiction.

Meanwhile, drifting below the ceiling, Gilda inspected the wires with a drill sergeant's eye for detail. Mrs. Hannity sought volunteers for the cleanup, Fast Eddie tried to get the coffeepot off the stacked chairs without anyone noticing, and Jingle Jim floated into a corner to compose a sonnet memorializing the fracas.

If a gnome could dislocate his jaw, I'm sure Gned's would've hit the floor. He was fascinated by the uproar, the bustle and the busyness, the advice given and the orders ignored. I knew he'd burst if I didn't turn my back so he could rearrange himself for a better view.

Cal drifted over. "There's no way we're going to have a worthwhile discussion in this room. Why don't we see if there's another place we can meet?"

Hank was arriving with a trio of newbies in tow who looked suspiciously like cheerleaders, although there might be some other explanation for their pom-poms and matching sweaters. I motioned for him to help me check the basement rooms.

The cheerleaders were downcast to see Hank leave, although morale picked up when the pigtail at the back of his *cafe au lait* neck waved goodbye.

Despite many meetings in the church, Hank and I knew little about the rest of the basement.

"Can you see yourself hunkered down in the furnace room?" I asked after a quick survey.

"It has more space than the storage rooms, the janitor's workshop or the restrooms," he said. "But the pilot light on the water heater would freak out our friends."

"We can't let that happen."

By the time we returned to the meeting room, the joint was packed. Gned had shifted to the top of a pile of folding chairs with the best view. Half the attendees were making suggestions to the other half, who were sorting out the useful suggestions they wanted to force-feed to everyone else.

I drifted into a corner. Whatever made me think that this bunch had the solutions that eluded me for so many sleepless days?

"Can I have some quiet to work?" Jingle Jim asked no one in particular.

"Not anymore," I said. "We're having a *group babble*."

Group babbles are what happens when a roomful of independent spirits try to reduce a universe of possibilities into a single clear, sharp-edged plan. Never a pretty sight.

Still, the discussion ended more quickly than most. An exasperated Fast Eddie announced that anyone who was serious about recovery was welcome to join him on the lawn. Veronica said she would host a meeting in the hallway, and it was everyone's responsibility to keep up with her.

Rosetta, meanwhile, would reconvene the one, true, authentic meeting in a side aisle of the church upstairs, while Cal crossed his arms over his chest and suggested that anyone who planned to get through the night without a *stumblie* had two minutes to haul their sorry little astrals to the lumberyard by the airport.

Gned and I watched the room empty in a ragged series of *poof, poof, poof* and a stream of *poofpoofpoofpoof* as the crowd departed for other parts.

I looked at Gned. He was wide-eyed at the rapid cascade of events.

"Welcome to my world," I said.

— End of Sample —

ACKNOWLEDGEMENTS

The author gratefully acknowledges the support of his writer's group buddies: Rebecca Ruark, Carol Rutherford and Barbara Weitbrecht.

Thanks to Bailey Hunter for a wonderful cover design and internal design.

Special thanks to my wife, Lee T. Budahn, for her support, humor and eagle's eye.

For the latest about the St. Sears group, check out our website at SpectersAnonymous.com.

Books in the Specters Anonymous series are available on Kindle and from Amazon.com.

Made in the
USA
Middletown, DE